FURTHER REDUCTION

This is a work of fiction. All names, characters, places, and events are creations of the author's imagination. Any resemblance to any actual person, living or dead, is purely coincidental.

Copyright © 2017 by Brian Cheatham
All rights reserved.

Printed by CreateSpace, an Amazon.com Company

ISBN 978-1-976-46826-1

Available from Amazon.com, CreateSpace.com, and other fine retail outlets.

This book is dedicated to my family and friends, without whose support and encouragement it wouldn't have been possible.

See what you made me do? ☺

Follow me online at
briancheatham.net

Special thanks to Duallogic and Pond5.com for cover art.

Further

Reduction

By

Brian Cheatham

Chapter 1

"Breathe. Now, let some of it out and hold what's left. Press the trigger, don't yank."

The rifle cracked loudly, shattering the morning silence.

"I think that was a good one. Let's go take a look," Mark Himes smiled at his daughter as she pulled the hearing protection off and laid the pink muffs beside the rifle.

"Okay," Ashley said with a massive grin on her face.

Her safety glasses almost gave her a cartoony sci-fi appearance. They weren't made for a child's head, but they were the only thing Mark could find this morning and some protection was better than none. He made a mental note to get a range bag together specifically for his daughter. At thirteen she was getting more interested in shooting with her father and showed some real promise as a marksman, or markswoman, as the case may be.

The pair left the bench and headed downrange to inspect the results. The third shot of the set was within an inch of the first two, making her total group size just over two and a half inches. Mark reached into his pocket producing a Sharpie marker and proceeded to number the holes in the target.

"I want to do it. It's *my* target," Ashley smiled as her father sheepishly handed her the marker.

"Not too shabby there, squirt," Mark commented, "Before long you may have to go hunting with old dad to make sure we have meat on the table."

Without hesitation she replied, "Not going to happen. I don't like to hunt."

"You like to eat, don't you?" Mark prodded the girl.

"Yes, but that doesn't mean I want to know where it comes from."

"You like to fish. What's the difference?" Mark continued, more curious to hear her rationale.

"But fish aren't cute like a deer, so it's OK to eat them." She capped the marker and handed it back to her father who smiled broadly at her train of thought.

"Well, I don't guess I can argue with that," he said, "Now that you are all sighted in, let's see what we can do about your math scores."

The duo returned to the bench and collected a stack of papers with numbers in large bold letters written across each sheet. They taped each page to a different target and then returned to the bench. Mark reached into his range box and produced a stack of index cards with mathematical formulas jotted down on them.

"You know the drill. Do the math and shoot the answer. You have one minute to pick your answer for each problem."

"Okay," she said as she snuggled up to the shooting bench again.

Mark laid a pencil and a scrap piece of paper on the table for her to work on, and then pulled up a chair beside her.

"Shooter ready?" He asked in an official sounding tone.

"Ready," came the reply.

Mark flipped the first index card out and showed the problem to his daughter. She jotted it down on the paper and began working the problem while Mark watched the clock.

Ashley quickly ciphered the problem out and circled the answer, slipped on her eye and ear protection and lined up for her shot.

Without a word, the rifle bucked and the round was away. Mark leaned in and checked the spotting scope to see where the round had landed. There, nearly dead center on the number "18" target, was a hole.

Mark looked down at the scrap paper and then to his daughter.

"Eighteen, huh? You sure about that?" He feigned looking down his nose as if he were an old schoolmarm peering over a fictitious pair of spectacles.

She cut her eyes over at him with a cautious smile and said questioningly, "Yes?"

He flipped the card over and displayed a large number 18 on the back.

"Nice job. You still had eight seconds to boot. Let's try something a little harder, shall we?"

Ashley grinned a satisfied grin and nodded enthusiastically, grabbing her pencil again.

After a dozen or so more calculations came break time. Mark returned to the bed of the truck and drew a pair of soft drinks out of the cooler in the back. He pulled his chair up again to the shooting bench, reclining as comfortably as the collapsible furniture would allow, and took a long slow sip.

"Daddy?"

"Hmm?"

"What do you do at the police department?"

The question caught Mark off guard so that he almost sat upright in his seat.

"Maintenance work. Why?"

"Oh, some of the kids at school were talking about their parents and their jobs and I just didn't really know what it is that you do now."

Ashley turned her attention back to her drink momentarily before continuing, "So, you're not *actually* a policeman?"

"No, no. I'm too old for that. They like younger folks to go to the academy."

"Is that because they aren't old and slow?"

Mark shot his daughter a sly glance as he lowered his bottle.

"What's that supposed to mean?"

Ashley smiled with a twinkle of mischief in her eyes that Mark had seen many times before from her mother.

"Nothing," she giggled, "Just that, you know, as people get older they can't run as fast. Or jump as high. Or drive as good. Or..."

"Yeah, yeah. Dig that hole a little deeper, girl. You didn't *really* want anything for Christmas this year, did you?"

She smiled again, then quickly finished off the drink and looked at her father.

"I'm glad you aren't a cop."

"Really? Why is that?"

"Because it's dangerous. You don't need to

be doing dangerous stuff like that."

With that she stood up and gave him as powerful a hug as she could, then made her way to the nearby restrooms.

Mark heard the door lock and thought to himself about what he really did do. As far as his family knew, he was a simple contract maintenance man for the department. He was called in to work on small things; change light bulbs, clean offices and mop floors if needed, and other light, menial tasks. To make it look good on paper, he was actually asked to do those things pretty regularly for a small salary. Mark didn't mind an honest day's work, but his main source of income was from the *other* contracting he did for the police.

For the past couple of years Mark had taken contracts known only to himself, Chief Dahlgren, and a mutual friend and officer, John Thompson, to rid the city of some of the worst criminals it had to offer. The conditions were that he couldn't tell anyone what he really did, not even family, and that his identity remain anonymous, even to the Chief.

Dahlgren had agreed to hire Mark openly as a part time maintenance man as a favor to John. He had no idea that Mark was actually his secret hired gun, code named "Specter." No other officers knew either, which made doing Mark's job a delicate balance. He was working for law enforcement, but also wanted by them for the work he did. Killing someone, even a scumbag, was, after all, still illegal.

Most of the time the jobs didn't bother him as much as the secrecy. He had always maintained strong communications with his wife, Angie, about everything. Now, he couldn't say anything about work. All of the dossiers about his targets had to be memorized and destroyed thoroughly and all evidence of the jobs cleaned up completely; before and after the trigger was pulled.

Mark's machine shop doubled as his war room. It was where he reviewed his information, planned out his jobs, and even designed, built, and sometimes tested his customized weapons and accessories. More than once he had fractured a law or two developing something that could help him pull off a job more effectively. Silence was golden and so suppressors were priceless. No traces meant no traces. His many years as an industrial machinist had given him the tools and skills to design and build most anything he set his mind to; given enough research material was available.

He took a long last swallow of the drink as the restroom door swung open and Ashley stepped back onto the range.

"Maybe, one day, it won't matter anymore and I can tell them what I really do," Mark thought. Until then, it was business as usual. And right now the business was getting Ashley back on the trigger.

"Everything come out alright?" Mark asked with a little chuckle.

"Dad!" Ashley's face flushed, "You're gross!" She grabbed her safety glasses and slipped them back on then reached across for her ear protection.

"Speed round time. Are you ready?"

"I guess. How do we do this again?"

"I read you a problem and you have to call, find, and shoot the answer within five seconds."

"Five seconds! I can't do that in five seconds!" Ashley's jaw hung open in surprise.

"Don't worry, they will be easy questions. Elementary school stuff. You still have to think quickly, though. Don't waste time. Are you ready?"

"OK, but I'd feel better if it was more than five seconds."

"Shooter ready?"

Ashley slipped the muffs over her ears and snuggled up to the rifle again.

"Ready."

"Two plus two."

Ashley cut her eyes across the stock toward her father in disbelief. Could this really be the format?

"Don't look at me. Think and fire. You just missed the first question."

She turned her attention back to the targets.

"Three plus one."

"Four!" She called as she pressed the trigger and sent a round into the corresponding sheet downrange.

"Nine minus three."

"Six" Another round raced away.

"Fifteen plus eight."

"Twenty three." The rifle belched again.

"Cutest boy in school."

"Tim…wait, what?" She looked over at her father who was grinning broadly.

"Thirteen plus six."

She hurried to get back on her sights and shouted, "Nineteen!" followed by, "That wasn't funny, Dad!"

"Focus," he snickered, "sometimes life tosses a lime in your lemonade. Nine plus nine."

"Eighteen." The shots continued to ring out.

"What's the capitol of New York?"

Ashley stammered for a minute, not expecting the subject matter to change.

"Uh, Albany."

"Good job.'

"I don't have a target for that."

"Just pick one. We're having fun."

They continued with the "ballistic study

hall" for most of the afternoon, then packed up their gear and headed for home.

When they walked in the door Mark immediately smelled dinner cooking. It was a favorite of his and Ashley's that Angie had come across on one of her Facebook sessions; fish with a white wine sauce. Despite sounding expensive, it was actually quite the opposite, especially when you caught the fish yourself and knew how to take advantage of the coupons and sales the way Angie did.

When Mark lost his job, they had learned quickly to live below their means. Cutting out luxuries meant more money at the end of the month and with Mark's hunting and fishing the cost of the groceries could be offset quite a bit. It wasn't comfortable, but it worked. They had managed to stay on top of things and even gain a little ground by being frugal.

"How are my two sharpest shooters doing?" Angie asked as Ashley plopped down at the table with her gear.

"I'm tired. Dad was like a drill instructor today."

Mark laughed. "You did fine. Keep your head clear and those math scores should be coming up in no time. You have the knowledge. Just don't get distracted."

Ashley nodded, then stood.

"I think I'm going to go take a bath. How long until supper?"

"Maybe 30 minutes. Take your time."

As Ashley rounded the corner and started down the hallway Angie turned to her husband.

"Did she really do well?"

"That girl is as natural a shot as I think I have ever seen," Mark began, "And yes, she did very well. Even when I tried to trip her up with trick questions, she handled it well."

"Good. I was worried that she just wasn't able to understand the math. That makes me feel better about things."

"She just needs to calm down before tests and clear her head. Stop paying attention to all the distractions and she'll be fine. I had the same problem back in high school. I nearly flunked Algebra One because of that girl that sat beside me after her gym class let out. With those tiny white shorts on and all, I couldn't concentrate on anything I was supposed to." Mark smiled broadly.

Angie turned again to him, a tinge of red to her cheeks, "As I recall those 'tiny white shorts' were just what I needed to get your attention back then."

"Oh, you already had my attention. That just made it undivided." He laughed as she grabbed him about the waist and pulled him down for a kiss.

Mark stepped out of her way to clear the range gear from the table and begin cleaning things up.

"Oh, one other thing," he said, "We need to listen for anything about someone named Tim."

Chapter 2

Miranda Ashcroft turned the lock on the front door to the bookstore and switched the sign from "open" to "closed" before making her way to the small room in the back of the building. There she collected a little bag with her exercise clothes inside and slipped off into the tiny bathroom nearby. She emerged a few minutes later in her yoga pants, running shoes, and a baggy tee shirt.

She stepped in front of a full length mirror that she had mounted to the back of the bathroom door and tied her auburn hair back in a pony tail. Around her waist she snapped a petite fanny pack that carried only the most essential items, namely her MP3 player and keys to get back in the shop when she finished her run. She also kept a small canister of pepper spray because, though she loved her bookstore, it wasn't located in the best of areas. Not the worst, mind you, but certainly not the best either.

In recent years the economy had been struggling and as a result crime had been on the increase. Burglaries and carjackings were on the rise everywhere and along with those property crimes inevitably came the violent crimes. She had seen the news reports on TV and in the papers and was well aware of just how violent people could be. She also knew that some didn't need to be provoked to attack; they were just naturally bent on doing harm to someone else.

After a few minutes of preparation, she stepped outside the back door of the small bookstore and started her run. The store was her pride and joy. A former IT professional, she was a very educated woman and even still enjoyed the occasional contract work that she gleaned in that field. At 30 she had already become disenchanted with the business and all the stress that came with it. That was when she decided to change gears and chase a dream.

Being savvy with her cash (a skill learned from her parents who were quite well to do in their own right) she had managed to purchase the bookstore building and slowly build it up over the past three years to its current state. Many people were surprised to learn that the attractive red head with her lean athletic build was actually a self-professed nerd through and through. She smiled to herself as she thought of the expressions she had gotten when her inner geek came out on a date.

Many men had felt deeply intimidated by her and so dates were few and far between. That didn't bother her much because she enjoyed spending time with her books and computers and her cat, Chauncey. He was the only male that stuck around with her and, frankly, the only one she really cared to see on a regular basis.

Her run took her down Fourth Avenue to the roundabout near downtown. From there she turned up Jefferson Street and followed the curving asphalt back around to Stratford which connected back to Fourth. The roughly triangular route allowed her to log about three miles and the last leg was predominantly downhill back to the store, which was always nice. She had hardly started her trek and she was already thinking about getting home and taking a hot shower before curling up with her latest book of choice.

Her progress to the roundabout was fairly quick and soon she was on Jefferson Street. She turned her music up slightly to keep her adrenaline going, but not enough to compromise hearing. Her new bone conducting head set was incredible for this because it didn't block the ambient noise, yet still provided amazing sound quality for the listening, unlike her old earbuds. With them in you couldn't hear someone right behind you and that could be a problem.

As she made the final turn back onto Fourth Avenue, her mind was focused on all the things to do the following day. She had ordered a new shipment of used books that were due in the morning. They would need to be inspected, logged into inventory, priced, and categorized on the shelves so that her customers could find them. There was also her internet sales that she needed to follow up on. That actually comprised the bulk of her sales since many of her available books were out of print and hard to find.

A few hundred more yards and she would be back at the shop. She slowed her pace and began a cool down walk for the last bit of the route. Running after work always left her tired, but she felt better for it and usually slept like a log afterwards. Chauncey appreciated that part as well since he liked to curl up at her feet each night.

Along the sidewalks, scattered among the street lights, bus stops, and shadows, Miranda could see the other side of the city taking shape. Homeless people for the most part, they typically came out after the businesses closed for the day and rummaged through the boxes and crates for whatever loot they could find. Anything of value was typically sold for alcohol of some sort, or perhaps a little companionship; whatever the immediate need was.

Two blocks from the shop Miranda turned off her MP3 player and was tucking the headband away when she got the sensation she was being watched. In this neighborhood, at this time of evening, that wasn't unusual. An attractive woman was often quite a spectacle compared to most others out here at the moment, but this was different. She glanced over her shoulder as she passed the end of the alley. To her relief there was nobody there. Turning her attention back to the sidewalk before her, she quickened her pace, anxious to reach the shop door. She almost ran headlong into the man that stepped out of the shadows in front of her.

Without a word he covered her mouth with a massive hand and began pulling her toward the alleyway. As she stumbled through the boxes and cardboard left by an ineffective garbage man, she felt the man's hot breath on her neck.

"Don't make a sound and this will all be over quick," the stench of cigarettes and whiskey flowed from his maw like a poisonous gas, "I've been watchin' you for a while, girl. We gonna have some fun tonight."

He pushed her down beside a dumpster where she fell on her hands and knees. As she looked back at her attacker she saw him step closer, his hands fumbling at his waist.

In the darkness a pair of muffled gunshots coughed from the alleyway followed by an uncanny silence.

"Got another one," John Thompson's voice carried through Dahlgren's doorway, breaking his attention from the computer screen.

"Homicide?"

"Yes sir," he stepped in the doorway as the chief leaned back in his chair. He nodded to Thompson to close the door for a little privacy.

"OK, let's have it."

"Male, Caucasian, age 44 found shot to death this morning beside a dumpster off Fourth Avenue. Two rounds, point blank to the chest. Never had a chance."

"Any witnesses?"

"Not a one, sir." Thompson sat down across the desk from his superior and laid the file on top of the mound of paperwork before him.

"Of course not. There never is."

Dahlgren rubbed his chin for a moment before continuing.

"Nine millimeter?"

"Yes sir."

"Any evidence, other than the body and bullets?"

"Nothing yet, sir. Forensics is still working the scene. All I have are the preliminaries."

Dahlgren turned to a large city map on the wall. The sheet was covered with various colored pins at points all across. It was Dahlgren's attempt at tracking crime in a very simplistic way. Each color represented a specific type of crime at a specific location.

"No witnesses and no evidence. Victim have any priors?"

"Yes sir. Repeat offender on many fronts. Assault, theft, battery, sexual assault, public drunk, DUI, the list is pretty long."

Dahlgren finally stood and made his way over to the map, selecting a pin as he stepped closer. He checked the address in the file and then firmly pressed the pin into the cork board. Then he turned back to Thompson and his chair.

"How many is this? Five? Six?"

"I think this one makes seven this year with the same M.O. Same caliber weapon, similar scene, similar victim, no witnesses, and no hard evidence to be found."

"Any chance this could be Specter? He hasn't gone into business for himself, has he?"

"No, sir. I don't think so. I've known him for a long time. It's just not his style."

"You don't think so, but you don't know so," Dahlgren continued, "Get in touch with him and make sure. He's been a valuable asset to us, but if he's going off on personal missions, it's time to reel him in."

"I understand, sir. I'll get in touch with him."

Thompson stood and turned toward the door.

"John," Dahlgren called.

"Yes, sir?"

"If it isn't him, we have another problem. One that might require his special…skill set."

"I agree. I'll keep you posted. Is there anything else?"

"No, son. Keep up with the field reports on these crimes and keep me in the loop on your other 'research' as well. I'll be interested to hear what you come up with."

Thompson nodded his head and closed the door behind him. When he reached his desk he considered calling Himes right then and there.

The Chief had a point. If Mark wasn't the one taking out these guys, someone else was. The reports almost looked like professional hits, but the victims were not big league people. Most of them were just your average lowlife trouble.

Robbery was never a motive either. All the victims were found in possession of their wallets and cash, if they had anything to start with, and identification still in pockets, untouched. No connections had been made between the victims either. No common associates or locations to speak of. They just didn't run in the same circles. It was random and yet, specific.

The fact that no shell casings or physical evidence had been found was disturbing also. Someone had taken great care to make sure that the scene was sanitized before leaving. That meant someone was careful. Not an easy task considering the shots were made at point blank range.

Thompson decided to look further and see if he could find anything in the way of a witness. A video camera or even a drunk in the corner would be better than nothing. He was familiar with the area, but not terribly so. There were no banks or ATMs nearby, so that ruled out his first preference for security camera footage. Perhaps some of the little shops and boutiques there would have something he could use. There was only one way to find out.

Before long John was en route to the crime scene. As he drove he again considered calling Mark. He really didn't want to call from his departmental vehicle, so he decided it was best to wait until he could have a more secure and quiet conversation.

He arrived on scene as the forensics team was packing the last of their gear. The crime scene tape was stretched like a giant yellow web around trash cans and street lights, one end already swimming in the morning breeze.

He slipped under the tape and flashed his badge to one of the crime scene investigators, a small fellow with wire rimmed glasses and short gelled hair.

"Good morning," came the reply, "You've missed all the fun."

"Yeah, I can see that. The Chief wanted me to come down and get some more information about what happened. Anything newer than an hour ago?"

"We found a few strands of red hair near the dumpster, but those probably belong to the girl that owns this store. She said she uses the back entrance here regularly when she opens and closes each day. According to her, she was long gone before time of death last night."

John looked the scene over, "Anythinig else?"

"Not yet. We've got the body already at the morgue and we'll begin examining finger nails for skin and hair, but as of right now it looks like someone just walked up to the poor slob and shot him for no reason."

"The girl, you said you already spoke to her?"

"Yeah. She owns this little bookstore here. She didn't see anything, but she's cooperative and willing to answer any questions since it happened right outside her shop. She's not hard to look at either," the technician smiled wryly at John and then returned to loading his equipment.

Thompson made his way to the front door of the shop and let himself in. To the left was a small cashier station and counter. To the right was a collection of tables and chairs for patrons to relax and read in. The smell of coffee infected the entire building and John immediately realized he hadn't had his morning pick me up yet.

Rows of shelves ran the breadth of the shop with books crammed into every possible space on them. Toward the center sat a small table with a handwritten sign on it announcing a sale on classic literature. It was covered with books all stacked neatly, despite the variety of sizes and bindings.

As John browsed lightly through the covers a voice called from the back.

"Just a minute. I'll be right out."

"Take your time, ma'am. I'm in no hurry."

True to her word, about a minute later Miranda stepped out of the back with both arms loaded down. The books were destined for the sales counter, but a couple didn't make it far into the room before slipping to the floor.

"Sorry. I'm a bit of a klutz. Let me put these down and I'll be right with you." She reached the counter and dropped the remaining load with a thud, then turned to pick up the stragglers that lay on the floor. John was a bit surprised at the young woman's appearance. She was everything he didn't expect to see as a bookstore owner.

As she placed the last books on the counter, Miranda turned her attention to the possible customer in her midst.

"Sorry about that. Is there something specific you were looking for?"

John smiled and produced his badge, "No, ma'am, I didn't actually come in for books. I was wondering if I could talk to you about what happened in the alley out back.

"Oh," she said with a start, "I already spoke to some officers earlier. Did they forget to ask something?"

"No, no, I'm sure they didn't and I'm sure you were very helpful. My chief wanted me to look into what happened and see if there was any security footage we might be able to access to help with the investigation. You don't have any cameras, do you?"

Miranda shook her head, "No, I've thought about putting some in, but just never got around to it. Now that this has happened, I'm REALLY thinking about it.

"As a matter of fact, I can't think of anyone in the neighborhood that has any kid of security system other than alarms. We're all small boutiques and specialty shops, so we run on tight budgets to start with. Security is kind of a luxury, to be honest."

"You aren't worried about anyone breaking in?"

Miranda laughed, "That's the one advantage to having a bookstore. Nobody wants to steal anything I have!"

He discussed the change in the neighborhood, especially after dark with her and gave her a few pointers on what she could do to help secure the facility cheaply, but effectively before wrapping up his interview.

"Thank you very much for your time. I hope I haven't been too much of an inconvenience."

"No, no. It was a pleasure. That other guy that was in here; the little one with the glasses? He gave me the creeps. I had to squat down a couple of times to keep his eye contact, if you know what I mean."

John laughed, "Don't feel bad. I thought I was going to have to squat to keep his eye contact too."

As he headed toward the door he handed her a business card.

"If you hear or see anything, I'd appreciate a call."

"Thank you," she quickly scanned the card, "John. And if you ever need a deal on a good book, you know where to find me."

Her smile was invigorating. John stepped back onto the sidewalk still stunned. *"I wonder if she's single,"* he thought to himself.

As he headed back to the station he decided it was time to grab some belated breakfast and give Mark a call.

Chapter 3

Mark stared at the computer monitor like he was decrypting a secret code to win a war. On the screen were a myriad of shapes and colors. Little icons surrounded the perimeter while pop up menus littered the right side of the display.

"I'll never figure this crap out," he mumbled to himself.

As a machinist for years, Mark was familiar with how to read prints and turn the drawings into reality, but Computer Aided Design was never a strength of his. He was computer savvy enough to understand what he wanted to do, and he was getting pretty close, but he was still learning this software and his patience was wearing thin.

Beside the computer, occupying a good portion of a small work bench, sat a 3D printer. He had set aside money for one so he could prototype designs out of plastic before committing to them in metal. He quickly realized that the thing could be useful for more than prototyping. He had successfully used it to produce replacement parts for broken appliances around the house., as well as toys for the kids, and even some office supplies that Angie was able to use at work. It had proven to be a very handy tool to have and there were thousands of files available online to print out that didn't require any design knowledge. Prototyping was another matter, though.

To help speed the design process, the manufacturer had incorporated a feature that allowed a photograph or sketch to be loaded as a background image. The designer could then trace out the shape and add thickness and contours until it became a three dimensional representation of the two dimensional image. The added benefit of turning the design into a printable model directly from the software was an extra bonus.

Mark was amazed at just how far technology had come for this type of thing since he first machined a part. There was even a module built into the software that allowed the design to have a tool path automatically created based on user input. If his home machining shop was advanced enough, he could actually program the little milling machine in the corner to machine metal directly from his design on the computer. It was light-years ahead of the manual programming of days gone by.

Of course, that was all possible if you knew how to use it in the first place. It had been years since Mark had actually worked in CAD and he struggled to remember what he could, then figure out how to transfer that knowledge into a usable format for the new program. Some of it worked, but the frustrating things seemed to be the simplest operations.

As he sat there, switching from the modeling page to the help page his phone rang. Without even glancing over he reached for the device and answered with an almost sleepy, "Hello?"

"Did I wake you up?" John sounded a little surprised at the groggy salutation.

"What? No. I'm sorry, man. I'm just a little distracted right now. Trying to learn some software. What's up?"

"Oh, sorry to bust your train of thought. Hey, will you have any free time today? I need to talk to you about something. I'd rather do it face to face."

Mark was completely involved in the conversation by this point.

"Yeah, I can pick this up later. When and where?"

"How about Chokichi Grill? Feel like some sushi?"

"I think I'll pass on that," Mark replied, "Never got over that Maguro Natto that time. Any place more…not raw… you'd care to eat at?"

John laughed at the mention of the raw tuna and fermented soybean dish that Mark had sampled on a dare a few years earlier. He never had much of a taste for exotic foods, and that one had almost completely turned him against trying anything new.

"OK, how about a sandwich from Charlie-Q's? Good barbecue and their ham always hits the spot. Plus, it's all cooked."

"I can do that. When?"

"Meet me in an hour? Will that work?"

Mark glanced at the screen again, "Yeah, I'm not gaining any ground at this right now. Maybe a break would be a good thing. See you in an hour."

The friends hung up and Mark began clearing up the pile of notes and printouts from the help pages that almost covered his desk. Maybe after a break he could get a fresh perspective on the program and things would click better.

An hour later and the duo were sitting on the patio of the restaurant with a pair of pulled pork behemoths in front of them. Charlie Q's wasn't fancy by any stretch of the imagination, but it was certainly the best barbecue joint in the area and had the trophies to back up the claim. What they didn't spend on atmosphere, they made up for in quality.

With a mouthful of sandwich, Himes managed to get a couple of intelligible words out.

"So, what's up?"

Thompson had to choke down a bite before he could reply.

"You know anything about a shooting last night around Fourth Avenue?"

"Nope. Should I?"

After swallowing another mouthful, Thompson carried on with the conversation.

"So, you didn't pull the trigger on a guy in a dark alley last night?"

Himes looked at his friend curiously.

"I didn't have any outstanding contracts to cash in on. Why would I have shot someone? Besides, I've spent every waking moment this week trying to learn that stupid program."

"Hmm," John grumbled, "Well, if you didn't that makes me feel better. And worse."

Now Himes was really getting confused.

"What's going on, John? Is there something I should know about?"

Thompson sat back in his chair and wiped a massive drop of the house sauce from his bottom lip.

"This morning we had a body show up in an alley over on Fourth. The victim wasn't a nice person, and someone didn't treat him very nicely either."

"OK. You have gang on gang violence all the time, remember? That's what a lot of my work has been about. Taking the big guys out to try and curb the growth."

"This wasn't a gang shooting. This dude was just plain old trouble. Not gang related. Someone walked up to him and plugged him twice with a nine millimeter in the chest. No brass. No prints. No witnesses. No evidence other than a body and two bullets."

Himes now sat back in his chair. No traces. That had always been the arrangement for his contracts.

"Professional hit?"

"I thought about that, but this guy doesn't make any sense. He's not an organized crime figure. He's not a gang member. He doesn't run in those circles. He's just a lowlife in general with a long history of doing stupid stuff to get into trouble."

"Man," Mark began, "I don't know. It wasn't me, I know that. It sounds like you have another hitter on the field."

"Well, it gets better," Thompson continued, "So far this year there have been seven hits like this, including this one. No known acquaintances between victims. No known associations or common locations. All found dead without witnesses or evidence. All shot point blank with a nine millimeter handgun.

"Chief was beginning to think you had gone into rogue mode and decided to clean up the city on your own. I told him that wasn't your style."

"Nah, I'm not *that* crazy," Mark smiled, "Well, not yet, anyway."

The two finished off their lunches and Thompson decided it was time to step the conversation up to the next level.

"Mark?"

"Yeah?"

"Do you think you could take the new hitter out? I mean, based on what information I can give you?"

Mark thought about it for a second.

"Well," he began, "What information you have shared with me right now isn't much to run on. I mean, there is no pattern to connect any dots, right? Basically you have seven dead bad guys and nothing to connect them except the shooter, apparently. That's not a lot to work with."

"But you can track animals through the woods, right? How different would it be to track this guy down?"

"Following the blood trail of an injured animal is TOTALLY different than this. There's a trail, to start with. You don't have that. Even if the animal isn't injured there are still signs that point to its presence; tree rubs, bedding, scat, *something*. Unless your man is peeing on the bodies or taking a dump at the crime scene, well, I don't see how I can possibly help you."

Thompson chuckled at the notion of their vigilante marking his territory.

"Ok. I just thought I'd ask. I know Dahlgren had mentioned using you to find the guy. I guess it's back to good old fashioned police work."

"Sorry, man. Looks like you're going to

have to earn your pay on this one," Mark smiled, "It is bothersome to see someone else doing my job, though. Especially when they are doing such a good job of doing my job."

"Looks like you've got a fan club, dude," Thompson quipped, "Never thought you'd have groupies."

Both men had a brief chuckle at the notion of a throng of dedicated followers chasing Mark's old pickup down the road from job to job as he dispatched bad guys all over town.

"Maybe you should go on the road and tour the worst neighborhoods across the nation," Thompson carried on, "The Dispensing Justice Tour."

"Yeah, maybe I could recruit this guy to be my opening act."

Both men again laughed at the absurd morbidity of the idea.

After a few minutes John changed the direction of the conversation.

"So, what's this software you've been trying to learn that has you so frazzled?"

"Oh, it's a new CAD program I downloaded a few days ago. Neat stuff, but it's a *lot* different than what I'm used to."

"CAD? What's that?"

"Computer Aided Design. I've been trying to get a grip on using it for some prototypes I want to build, but it's taking me a while to figure it out."

"Oh, I thought if it was an office suite I could help you out, but I don't know anything about that stuff.

"Trying to develop more 'hushpuppies,' are we?" John was referring to Mark's growing inventory of suppressors he had built for contracts. Since he couldn't have any traces back to him, he couldn't buy a suppressor legally. So, he figured out how they worked through a *lot* of research and made his own. His designs proved to be as effective as any of the name brand models, after some very uncomfortable field testing, of course. But they were cheaper to build and had no paper trail. Two items that were high on Mark's list.

"Actually, I think I'm good there for now,"

Mark smiled, "I've been looking into ways to break down faster and carry more compactly. That's always been an issue. I can't just stroll around with a full sized rifle slung over my shoulder and a pistol won't reach out like I need it to."

"So you want to be able to break it down smaller so it will be less noticeable? That makes sense."

"More than that, if I can get the overall length down to start with, I can carry easier still. I've been looking into bullpup designs a lot and I think I have an idea I want to try out."

"Bullpup? That's the one where the trigger is in front of the receiver, right?"

"Right. There are a lot of manufacturers out there producing bullpup style rifles, shotguns too, but nothing like a sniper configuration and caliber."

John scratched his chin for a second, contemplating the idea.

"Well," he finally said, "I wish I could help you there, but I'm no firearms expert. You clearly have more experience there than I do. Looks like

I'm totally useless to you today."

Mark chortled again.

"I know that John Garand, the inventor of the M-1 Garand, looked into a bullpup configuration for it following World War 2, but I don't know much about how it was designed or if it worked. I wish I could find some more information out about it. Maybe find a resource for weapon designs. Especially stock building. I'd like to make a custom stock for one of my rifles, but I have no idea where to start."

"I'm sure you could order something online. There are a ton of books out there on the net."

"Yeah, I thought about that, but I don't want my card tied to anything like that. If I could find a book I could pay cash for, that'd be great."

"I might have a solution for you," John dug through his pocket and found the scrap sheet that held the address for Miranda's shop on it, "This is the owner of the bookstore I interviewed this morning about the dude in the alley. He was found outside her back door. She might be able to hook you up with something."

Mark took the paper and glanced at the name and address.

"Okay. I'll swing by there today. I appreciate it." Mark tucked the paper away in his shirt pocket.

"Oh, before I forget," John leaned across the table, "If she's single, I call dibs."

Both men smiled before Mark replied, "I don't think you have anything to worry about. Angie wouldn't like it if I brought home a new lady friend."

Chapter 4

Mark drove through the neighborhood on Fourth Avenue, rubbernecking from side to side in an attempt to find Miranda's shop. John hadn't listed the name of the business, only an address, so he slowly cruised the area looking for street numbers. As he did, he collected quite a caravan of irate drivers behind him who didn't hesitate to tell him exactly what they thought of his driving.

Finally, nestled among the coffee shops and craft boutiques, he spied large letters spelling "Books" on the front of a building. He immediately made for the closest parking space and pulled in. As he shifted the truck into park he glanced at the rear view mirror in time to see one of his dedicated followers flip him off as the stranger accelerated away.

"Man, sometimes I really hate people," Mark sighed, and stepped out of the vehicle. He looked to the right of the building and noted the alleyway that was most likely the crime scene. To the left was a small florist. Above the door was a simple awning and the name of the business; Paper Works. On the picture window to the right of the door was the oversized lettering he had noticed earlier. Beside the door was the address number and it was a match. He could smell a faint wisp of coffee on the sidewalk, but couldn't tell where it was coming from at first.

Through the glass he noticed a single lady, probably in her late fifties to early sixties, with short brown hair and a pair of round rimmed glasses sitting in a chair and drinking a cup as she read an old leather bound book of some sort.

"John, if that's Miranda, we really need to talk about your eyesight," Mark thought as he reached for the door. He stepped inside and was about to ask the woman if she was the one John had spoken to when a voice called from off to his left.

"Good afternoon! Can I help you find anything?"

Mark turned, a little startled, to see a striking young lady with flowing auburn hair coming up the aisle toward him.

"You must be Miranda," Mark said, "I'm Mark, Mark Himes. My friend John was in here this morning about the incident in your alley. He gave me your name and address and told me to see if you could help me with something."

"Yes!" She smiled, "Of course. He seemed like a pretty nice guy. I'd be happy to help if I can. What is it you need?"

Mark glanced over at the lady in the chair, unsure if she needed to hear his business or not.

"Well, I'm a bit of an outdoor nut and I wanted to do some work on a hunting rifle I have. I was wondering if you had any books on gunsmithing or stock building I could take a look at. I'm really interested in a composite build because it isn't as susceptible to moisture and swelling."

"Hmm," she studied for a minute, "Guns, huh? Let me think."

"Miranda?" the lady had risen from her chair and moved to the cash register. Mark was surprised at how much she favored the little fashion designer from *The Incredibles*.

"Excuse me, please," Miranda whispered as she headed for the counter.

"I think I'll be taking this one home, dear," the little woman said, "It's not every day you come across one this old in this good of condition."

"That's what I thought as well. I'm glad to know you're the one buying it. I know it will be well taken care of in your library."

Miranda rang up the sale and the little woman headed out the door.

"Literature professor at the college. That woman has a library that would make the one in D.C. jealous. She's a little strange, but a sweet lady. Even if she does favor Edna Mode a bit."

Mark laughed out loud at the comment.

"I'm sorry," he giggled, "I was just thinking the exact same thing."

Miranda walked back over to John and said, "Follow me. I have a selection of books down here that are all about guns and other weapons. It's interesting stuff, but most of my clients are more interested in classic fiction or poetry."

"The only poem I can remember is Jabberwocky," Mark muttered.

"Ever hear it in German?"

Mark was surprised that she heard his comment. He didn't realize he had said it so loudly.

"Uh, no. Not that I can recall anyway."

"It has a really different sound, believe me," she smiled.

"How would that work? Do they have words like those in German?"

"Most of the words Lewis Carroll just made up for the poem, so there isn't a precedent in any language for them. When it was translated the real words remained but the silly words were changed to sound different in the translated version as well.

"For example, in the translation I know, Jabberwock is translated as Zipferlock. Bandersnatch is changed to Schnatterrind. The real words remain as they normally would."

"Wow," Mark said, "I never thought about that." He did think about how John might regret calling dibs since she was probably a lot smarter than he was.

"Here we are," Miranda said, gesturing to a section of books like she was a model on a game show, "If you can't find anything, let me know and I'll see if I can order something for you."

"Oh, okay Thank you," Mark said as he eyed the dozens of manuscripts in the section.

"Would you like some coffee while you do your research? On the house."

"Oh, no, I don't want to impose."

"No trouble. After all, any friend of John's…" She let the comment trail off as she headed for the front of the store.

Mark started to decline, but she was already gone. He scanned the spines and covers of the books before him, hoping something would jump out and scream, "What you're looking for is in here!"

His eyes finally settled on an older book about gunsmithing. He slipped it off the shelf and flipped to the table of contents. Sure enough, there was a section on stocks. It probably wouldn't contain anything about bullpups, but maybe there would be something he could use on how to build a stock anyway. He could use the techniques to build different designs. He just needed to know the techniques.

From what he saw there was ample information on design, which was helpful, but nothing about composites. He could use the information for length of pull calculations and the like, though, so he set it aside and continued to look.

One by one he pulled a small selection from the shelves and piled them on a table for further review. Miranda had returned with a massive steaming hot cup of coffee.

"Having any luck?"

"Possibly. I haven't seen any one book with the information I'm looking for, but each of these may have a little something I can use."

Mark sat down in the chair and took the coffee from his hostess, who then pulled up a chair on the opposite side of the table.

"Man," Mark said after a long sip, "that hits the spot. Thank you. Again."

"No trouble at all. I have some scones, if

you would like one."

"Thank you, but no. John and I just had a huge lunch and I'm afraid if I eat anything else I might explode. I appreciate the offer, though."

Miranda smiled as she leaned over the table looking at the stack of books before Mark.

"What kind of rifle are you working on?" She asked, point blank.

"Um, well, it's a Savage 10 model. That's a bolt action rifle."

Miranda cut her eyes up and met Mark's.

"Yes, I know. What caliber do you run it in? I'm guessing probably .308?"

Mark leaned back in the seat a bit, surprised at her apparent knowledge of firearms.

"Yes, it is, actually. I thought about going with a .30-06 when I was shopping because, well, I guess I'm a bit nostalgic and I've always liked the '06 round."

"Ah," she said, "That's a good solid caliber. Versatile too, if you can handle the kick. You can hunt a lot of things with it."

"I'm sorry; I didn't mean to sound, well,

like an arrogant know-it-all. Most women I know couldn't possibly care less about firearms, let alone know anything about them. I have to say, I'm impressed."

Miranda laughed, "Didn't expect that from a stuffy little librarian, did you?"

"No, no I didn't," Mark smiled again.

"Oh, I'm full of surprises," She said, "I grew up in Colorado. My family had investments in a lot of things, oil mainly, so we had a huge ranch and where there are ranches, there are animals. We used to hunt and fish and have to keep predators under control all the time. My father had three Remington 700's in different calibers for different reasons. One was in .30-06."

"Well, now I understand why John was so talkative about you. You are quite an impressive lady."

"Thank you," she replied, "Hang on a sec. I think I may have a new book in the back that might be of use to you."

She quickly stood and made for the small store room at the back, returning a couple of minutes later with a rather large book in hand.

"I got this in with my latest order today. It's not exactly a 'gun' book, but you wanted to know about composites, so this might help."

She laid the tome on the table and Mark instantly saw it was a book about how to work with fiberglass and composites. It covered everything from mold making to finish and paint.

"Hey! That might work!" he blurted out, "I didn't think about looking for something like that."

"See? I'm full of surprises."

Mark flipped through the pages of one, then another, setting some to the left and some to the right of the table, trying to decide which contained the most valuable data. Miranda watched him process his selection quietly for a few minutes before changing the subject entirely.

"So, are you an officer too?"

"Hmm? Oh, no. John and I have known each other for years. I do work for the department, but I'm not a cop."

"You work for the police department, but

you aren't a policeman? How does that work?"

"I do contract work. Mostly maintenance and some…janitorial stuff from time to time."

"I see. So you weren't here this morning, then."

"Oh, no. I was actually at home trying to learn a new software program."

"Really? What were you trying to learn?"

"It's a CAD program. That's…"

"Computer Aided Design, yes, I know," a sly smile crept across her face again.

"Well now I just feel embarrassed," Mark said, "You know computers too."

"Information Technology was my career before I got burned out and decided to chase the dream you see before you," she giggled as she gestured with her hands to the shelves and walls around the room, "I still do a little contracting of my own from time to time."

"Amazing," he said, "Is there anything you haven't done?"

Miranda sat back in the chair again, studying Mark's face.

Further Reduction

"I'm sorry, but you look very familiar. I can't figure out where I should know you from."

"Well, I don't think I'm on any wanted posters anywhere. It's been a while since I had my picture in the paper. Maybe we passed each other at the grocery store?"

"Wait," she said, a sudden expression of revelation across her face, "The paper! That's it! You are the guy that beat up the robber at that restaurant a few years ago!"

"Oh, yeah," Mark smiled, a little embarrassed by the sudden fame, "That was me. I'm surprised anyone remembers that."

"Yeah, I remember seeing it in the paper and then they had it on the news that night too. The guy was wanted for shooting someone. A cop?"

"Yeah, he and another guy had a robbery go wrong and his partner was killed. That guy was trying to get out of town and decided to hold up the restaurant for some spending money before he left.

"It just happened to be the same day I decided to try a fast food chain. I normally avoid those places like the plague."

Miranda laughed at the irony, "So, do you ever go back there to eat?"

"Nope. Never again. The overrated food just isn't worth the publicity."

The pair had a good laugh and then Miranda asked for details about what happened. Mark explained the move he used to disarm the man and showed her a quick demonstration.

"That looks like a Krav Maga technique," she said, "Is it?"

"Seriously? Yes, it is. Do you take Krav?"

"I took it for a few years, but my IT schedule got so busy I couldn't keep it up. I still practice what I learned, but I never picked it back up. There always seems to be something else to do, you know?" she paused momentarily, "Do you study it?"

"No, actually John is the one that showed me what little I know. He goes pretty regularly and works out at the studio, but I've never been."

Miranda casually dropped her gaze to

Mark's left hand. There was the wedding ring. It figured he would be married. She decided to shift gears on the conversation.

"Wow, John seems to be an interesting guy. His wife must be one lucky lady."

Mark saw where the comment was going.

"Oh, he's not married. He's not even dating anyone right now. Unless you count his job, I mean. That keeps him pretty busy."

"Really?"

Mark could see the wheels turning and decided to push the subject a little more.

"I'm sure if the right girl came along he would probably make it a point to back off on the work schedule. Right now it's just all he has to do. I think he keeps it up to avoid being bored."

Miranda was very tempted to ask bluntly if he could set her up with John, but she didn't want to seem too eager…or desperate.

"You know," Mark began again, "I'd say you two would make a good couple. If you were single, I mean."

"Oh, I'm single," she snapped back. Then

she worried that it might have been exactly the response she didn't want to make.

"I mean, well, oh, screw it. Do you think he'd be interested in going out some time?" There it was. Her desperation laid bare before a practical stranger. Inwardly she cringed at her own behavior, but still, the deed was done.

Mark chuckled, "I happen to know that John would be *very* interested in an opportunity to spend time with you. As a matter of fact, I think he was hoping you were single as well. If you'd like I can have him give you a call. I'm sure it wouldn't take much to twist his arm." He had never considered himself to be much for matchmaking, but when it was this obvious, even a novice like himself couldn't do much to mess it up.

Mark ended up with three books that day; the old gunsmithing book, the one about working with fiberglass and composites, and a third one dealing with general firearm design. All three were used, some a little more than others, but they all contained information he could use. Miranda suggested a little online research like YouTube. If a 10 year old could learn to drive to McDonald's with it, surely he could find out how to make a custom rifle stock.

Miranda also jotted down his name and phone number in case she came across anything else that he might be able to use. Mark worried that she might use it to pester him if things didn't work out between she and John, but that was a risk he figured was minimal.

Now it was time to get back home to meet the family…and try to learn that infernal software.

Chapter 5

When Mark called John to let him know Miranda was single, he first had to antagonize a bit.

"Hey, man. I just left the bookstore and are you in luck. I spoke to your woman there and she is really interested in you. She said if you would like to go out sometime that would be great with her."

Mark could almost hear the smile spreading across his friends face.

"Are you serious? She actually said that?" John's excitement was growing by the second.

"Sure did," Mark carried on, "I never thought you'd be interested in someone like her, though."

The line went silent momentarily.

"What? Why? Did you not see her? She's awesome!"

"Yeah, she's nice and all, but I didn't know

you were into short brunettes with coke bottle glasses and boyish haircuts. Whatever turns you on, brother. Oh, I told her you could meet her tonight at Victoria's at 7:30, so go wash the stink of justice off. You guys have fun."

"Wait, what? That's not what she…"

"Well, I'm going to have to let you go. Let me know how it all goes. Adios, man!"

Mark hung the phone up and laughed out loud at his mischief. The opportunity to get a cheap jab in at John didn't present itself often, so when it did he relished it. Maybe a little more than he should.

Almost immediately Mark's phone rang. Knowing it was John calling to correct him on his efforts at playing Cupid, he didn't even look at the screen before answering.

"What?"

The phone was silent for a moment before a feminine voice came on.

"Mark?"

The smile quickly vanished as he tried to figure out who it was.

"Yeah?"

"Okay, hey, this is Miranda. Did I catch you in the middle of something?" The sound of concern was crisp and clear in her voice.

Mark laughed a little, "No. Well, yes. I'm in the middle of tormenting John about going out with you, but other than that, no. What's going on?"

She laughed a little.

"What have you done?"

Mark explained how he had John thinking he was going to be meeting the little woman from the bookstore for dinner that evening and they both had a good laugh about it.

"That is so mean," she said with a giggle, "That's hilarious. He won't get mad, will he?"

"I've known John for years. He loves a good gag, even when he's the butt of it. He'll be fine once the initial shock of it wears off."

"Oh, good. I wouldn't want our date night to be ruined before it got started."

Mark backed up a bit and restarted the conversation.

"What's up? Did I forget something at the store?"

"No, no. I was thinking about your interests and decided to do a little digging around. I may have found a book that will help a lot. It's a 'comprehensive resource for firearm customization' according to the description I have. It's supposed to cover, in detail, all the facets of designing and building custom stocks, grips, heat shields and other furniture for rifles and shotguns and even has a large section on how prop masters will customize a weapon for a movie production to look like something it isn't while it still functions like a real weapon."

"That sounds like what I'm looking for. Can you order it for me?"

"I sure can. I'll have it before the end of the week."

"Thanks, Miranda, you're awesome. I'll swing by and pay you tomorrow, if that's okay. What's the damage?"

"We'll call it $25 out the door and you can pay me when it comes in. Fair enough?"

"Fair enough. I appreciate the help."

"My pleasure, Mark."

"Oh, before I forget, John is going to meet you at Victoria's tonight at 7:30. You might want to call and make sure he will be there." Mark giggled once again.

"Don't worry," she said with a grin, "I'll take care of it."

To say John was nervous was a bit of an understatement. Miranda had called while he was tied up in an interview with a suspect and left him a voice mail. She said Mark had told her about the time and location and that she would meet him at the restaurant at 7:30. He got so wrapped up in paperwork that he almost didn't have time to get ready for the date.

John didn't go out much. He spent a lot of his time at the precinct, working on cases and gathering evidence. Talking to people was the least glamorous part of the job, so he often let calls go to voice mail even if he wasn't busy. The suspect's family would call and berate him for having their loved one locked up when they were obviously innocent of ever having done anything wrong. Then the victim's family would call and he would again be raked over the coals for not working hard enough to bring them justice. Inevitably, when the time came for witnesses to testify, nobody, on either side, saw or heard anything. They didn't want to get involved.

Most nights all the frustration left him wanting to go to the gym and hit the punching bags, or just go home and sleep. Dating didn't fit into the schedule often.

He arrived early, as he was prone to do, and the host showed him to his table right away. He had mentioned that there would be a young lady meeting him and the host agreed to send her right over when she arrived.

After a few moments, the host again was at his table, but this time with a short brunette at his side. She was in her mid-fifties to early sixties with round rimmed glasses sporting incredibly thick lenses. John's jaw dropped slightly as the gentleman turned and left for the entrance and his post.

"You must be John," the lady said with a broad smile, "It's a pleasure to meet you. I've heard quite a bit about you." She pulled up a seat directly across as John stammered for words.

"Uh, yes. I'm uh, I'm John and I believe you have me at a total disadvantage." He smiled nervously trying not to offend the woman, but wondering who she was nonetheless.

"I'm your date for the evening, dear," she said without a hint of joking in her voice or on her face, "We were supposed to meet here at 7:30, weren't we?"

John was at a total loss. He didn't want to be rude, but he had no desire to follow through with a complete stranger for the evening. What had happened to Miranda? Where was his stunning redhead?

He glanced back to the door and across the room, his gaze finally coming to rest on the face of his dinner companion. She sat there smiling like the cat that ate the canary.

"Is something wrong, dear? You look a bit

stressed."

John mustered his most calm and civil tone, "No, nothing at all. I must admit, I was expecting someone else, though." He glanced sharply back toward the door. Mark had something to do with this. He had to.

"I see," she began, "Do you want me to leave?"

"What? No. No. Of course not," John said, "I just, um, I, uh. Have you made your mind up for what you'd like?"

The lady just sat there smiling and giggling quietly to herself behind her menu. John directed his attention to his own menu and was trying to figure out how best to get Mark back for the situation. He was totally oblivious to the person standing at the table across from him.

When he finally lowered the menu he looked across to see Miranda standing there with a devilish grin across her face and the little woman still seated at the table and still laughing.

"Thank you, Helen. I'll take it from here," Miranda said with a laugh.

"It was my pleasure, dear. I haven't had a good laugh at someone else's expense in a while." With that, she stood up and smiled at John, taking his hand in hers and, with the most sincere expression in her eyes said, "Perhaps another time, John. I'm afraid it just wouldn't work out between us right now."

She gave Miranda a hug and was quickly gone. Miranda assumed her seat at the table and smiled at John, disarming him immediately.

"You?" The surprise was complete, "You did this?"

Miranda laughed out loud at his sudden grasp of the situation.

"I'm sorry. I had to. Mark told me about your conversation and I just had to. He said you could take a joke. I hope he wasn't lying."

John slumped back in the chair.

"No, you got me. Fair and square, you got me. I was thinking of all the ways I was going to pay him back and now I have to figure out how to get *you* back."

They both enjoyed the aftermath of the

prank and the rest of the evening that followed.

John was entranced by not only her radiant beauty, but her intelligence as well. She was incredibly well rounded and educated, yet she was a prankster and a nerd at the same time.

Miranda was intrigued with John's protective nature and his casual attitude. He was serious about taking care of people he cared about and he pushed himself to develop the skills to do just that. At the same time, he was so laid back and loved to joke around. While he didn't have an ivy league education, the passion he had for his profession and the impact he made on the lives of his community more than made up for it.

Had it not been for their work schedules, the conversation might have lasted all night. John quipped that he might call in sick the next day, just to have an excuse to stay out and learn more about her. In the end, they decided to set up another date and resume their talk then. Both went home grinning like idiots.

Further Reduction

The following morning, John called Mark and covered the entire evening's affair. Mark cackled when he told about Miranda's set up with Helen, the woman from the shop. Miranda had offered to buy the woman's dinner in exchange for her participation, but Helen had flatly refused any compensation other than being party to the prank.

Mark asked if they would be seeing each other again and he said that they were. His schedule was more problematic than hers and he was looking at best options while talking to Mark.

"Hey, I'll tell you what," Mark began, "Why don't you two come over to the house this Saturday evening? We'll cook out and she can meet my family. I'm sure they would love to meet her and it would be a cheap night out away from the city. What do you say?"

"That sounds like it could be fun. I'm in if she is. I'll call her in a bit and let you know what she says."

"Well, alright then, we have half a date going anyway," Mark joked.

"Thanks, man. I appreciate it. Let me

know if you need us to bring anything."

"No worries there. We've got it covered."

John decided that he needed to get a little business done while he had Mark's attention.

"Not to change the subject, but, well, to change the subject…"

"Got some work for me to do?" Mark's tone got a little more intense.

"Yeah, maybe. First off, have you had any luck finding that part we asked about?" John was, of course, referring to him finding the vigilante. Mark assumed his friend was in at least a public place, probably the precinct and didn't want to openly discuss their contracts.

"No," he said, "Nothing yet. I started mapping all the points you told me about, but I haven't gotten anywhere on it yet. If you come across any more information, shoot it to me. More is better."

"Will do. Secondly, I may have some more work to send your way. Do you have some time to meet me and talk about cost and timing?"

That was John's way of telling him they

had a contract hit ready and he wanted to give the information to Mark along with the price. The chief and John had worked up a rough pricing schedule for various bounties based on what charges were pending, or what arrests had been made that the person was able to wriggle out of. Certain variables made the base price higher or lower, depending on their wrap sheets, so no two jobs were ever exactly the same.

"Sure," he replied, "How long have you got?"

"We can talk about it over lunch. No real rush. You decided where this time."

The friends met at Rachel's, a locally owned burger joint that had what Mark considered the best hamburgers in town. He wasn't alone. They were famous for being large, juicy burgers that were cooked to order and loaded with whatever fresh toppings you cared for. The only thing better than a Rachel's burger was a massive order of the French fries. Mark preferred them with a light coat of their house made seasoning salt for a little extra spice. With or without, they were delicious. If you left that establishment hungry, it was your own fault.

"So, what have you got for me today?" Mark asked as he sat his glass back on the table.

John leaned across the table, sliding a plain manila folder across as he did so.

"This gentleman is our concern. He doesn't look like much, but looks can be deceiving. At 28 years old, he has climbed the ranks of one of the area gangs and established himself as a very important person with suspected cartel connections."

Mark opened the folder and looked the mugshot over carefully. The man's appearance was not imposing. He was of a slight build and not terribly tall. In the photo you could clearly see the teardrop tattoo on the corner of his right eye and a few ink patterns on the neck. He had a lengthy history and ran in some of the areas Mark had worked. The chances were decent that Mark may have actually had the man in his sights before.

"Cartel? As in drug cartel?" Mark never looked up from the dossier.

"Drugs, weapons, human trafficking, and a host of other hobbies. They've been trying to get a strong foothold in the area for years and this guy is a key to that. He's not their only option, mind you, but right now he seems to be their primary."

"Okay," Mark replied as he closed the folder, "Any preferred hangouts? Common areas of interest? Anything I can use for a vantage?"

John leaned back in his chair, "There are some things you need to know first. This isn't going to be a walk in the park."

Mark looked a little concerned.

"It never is. That's why I don't rush into things. That's one reason why you asked me to do this job, remember?"

"I know, but this isn't our local flavor gang strike. These guys have deeper pockets and better resources. That makes them harder targets. Even the lower members."

Mark looked again at the information packet before him. He had worked in the area before, but this particular person seemed to isolate himself more than his prior hits; maybe because of Mark's effectiveness.

"I'll probably stick out like a sore thumb in the neighborhood," he muttered.

"Don't be too sure about that," came John's response.

"How do you mean?"

"Well, normally, gangs rally around something the members have in common, like race or nationality. These guys are more diverse. They're united by money and power. They are beginning to realize that sometimes you need a white guy to do something and sometimes you need a Hispanic. The defining factor is the accomplishment of the task, not the race of the individual. Same thing goes for gender. Sometimes, you just need a woman's touch."

"So they recruit along all lines? That's a very politically correct way to run a gang," Mark smiled.

"You'd better believe it. Strength through diversity. A lot of members have military experience on top of it all. Some even have law enforcement history. These boys and girls are the real deal, Mark. We have to be careful here."

"You think this is where old Rat Face was making his money?" Mark was referring to an older case that resulted in the arrest of a former military armorer who had made his money modifying weapons for criminal use. During the raid, the police managed to confiscate a large number of illegally modified guns and even some military grade explosive materials.

"At least some of the stuff, yes. Watch your step, man. Take your time. If it's too much, let me know."

"Give me a few days to look into it. I'll let you know what I decide. Will that work?"

"Sounds good to me."

Chapter 6

After a few days of Google Earth and a lot of map study, Mark called John and told him he thought he had an approach that might work. He would need to get a first hand look at the area, though and that meant boots on the ground.

Since most of the active crime in the area was during evening into the early hours of the morning Mark decided that he would park at the garage on 17th Avenue and walk in before sunrise. The garage was as close as he could reasonably get without actually parking a strange vehicle in the area. That might rouse suspicion.

If he walked in around 4:00 in the morning, most of the neighborhood activity should be minimal. Still, he would be carrying his faithful 1911 along with his duffle bag.

Inside the bag, Mark typically packed a small carbine and spare magazines, then covered them with smelly socks and underwear. If someone decided to take a look, they would at least have to deal with that layer first. The carbine wouldn't be as easily retrieved as the pistol, but he hoped he wouldn't have to use it either. A little lower in the bag he carried a plastic pouch of spare clothes from a thrift store to change into, if he needed to blend in a little more.

This trip would be slightly different. Mark had modified the duffel to include a tear open pocket on the outside that he could stuff magazines in. The hook and loop strips held it firmly closed, but tore open easily enough to make it a quick access point. He kept a small neoprene face mask in there as well to help conceal his identity. It was warm, but the item covered his neck, chin, mouth, and nose well enough to keep his identity secret. Mark thought the screen printed skeletal jaw design on it added to the "cool" factor.

Thanks to Robert Deevers, a high school friend who ran a reasonably successful body shop, Mark was able to line the interior of the bag with a couple of layers of Kevlar fabric. It wasn't bullet proof, but it was bullet resistant enough that he felt a little safer carrying it into areas like this. If the truth were told, it probably wouldn't slow a serious round down at all, but he preferred not to think about it too much.

Instead of tucking his carbine away in the duffel bag, Mark had opted for a tiny AR-15 that he had cobbled together. He used a pistol upper half assembly with a quick detach barrel mated to a standard lower receiver. The stock was attached with a side folding hinge setup that allowed the entire gun to be carried under a jacket or, if the situation demanded it, under a very large, loose fitting shirt.

He chose to configure it for the 300 Blackout cartridge by Advanced Armament Corporation since it was designed to be suppressible from the start. AAC was well known as a suppressor manufacturer before they began designing their own ammo and the combination was hard to beat. He tucked one of his own custom suppressors inside the duffel bag pocket to go along with the load out, just in case he needed to work quietly. To finish it off, the top rail was equipped with a holographic sight. If you could see the dot, that was where the bullet would go. Quick and accurate.

The weapon was totally illegal since it was a clear violation of the National Firearms Act, but so was the suppressor, and the job itself.

"Go big or go home," Mark thought to himself as he tucked the tiny weapon under his left shoulder into the homemade holster. It wasn't pretty, but he could get the weapon out and assembled in less than seven seconds when he pushed himself. Fast enough on the range, but that could mean life or death in a bad situation.

Mark pulled into the parking garage a little after 2:30 a.m. and began his hike in. By the time he reached the neighborhood the entire area was eerily dark and silent. From time to time he would scare up a stray cat or large rat rummaging through the dozens of garbage cans on the streets. Otherwise it was silent. He found the abandoned church building he was looking for and slipped across the yard to the rear. It wouldn't give him the lofty vantage point he preferred to take a shot from, but he wasn't there to take a shot. Not yet, anyway.

At the rear of the church he dug into his pocket and produced a small night vision monocular. It wasn't as fancy as the equipment the police department had, but he didn't have access to that kind of budget. All he needed was to make sure he wasn't walking into an opium den or crack house full of addicts on his way to scout the target.

He slipped it up to his eye and allowed the infrared floodlight on the side to do its job. Now bathed in invisible light, the church yard came into focus without a soul around. Carefully, Mark scanned the neighborhood and then made his way to the back door of the building.

In its day, the old structure was probably a beautiful example of architecture. Tall stained glass windows still occupied most of the frames, albeit many were now missing; shattered by rocks and beer bottles. The woodwork was actually very well crafted and assembled. Himes thought to himself what a shame it was that the life of the old building was gone. Certainly this neighborhood could use a little of what used to be offered here.

He finally managed to make it into the

building and find the stairway to the balcony level. From outside he had noticed a large hole in one of the windows facing the target area. He should be able to sit comfortably back on the balcony with his spotting scope and monitor the area without much worry of being seen.

He found an old straight backed chair and pulled it over toward the window to get comfortable. He would only have a couple of hours before sunrise and he wanted to get back to his truck before then. Time to get to work.

Himes noted the distance via the range finder in the spotting scope and jotted it in his pocket sized note pad. The street ran 820 yards straight into the front door of an old movie theater. Inside the theater was ground zero.

Even at this time of morning, Mark could make out activity at the building, but due to the low lighting conditions, he couldn't be sure what was going on. The monocular wasn't nearly effective at this distance, and the sky was overcast, so there wasn't any ambient light to silhouette anyone against. Still, he could see people on the sidewalk out front moving to and from the shadows from the street lights.

From what he could tell, there were at least three people out at the time. A possible fourth appeared momentarily at the right side of the building, but he couldn't be sure. He noted physical descriptions of each individual in his book as well as vehicles he could see, other structures and anything else that might be of value along with ranges for several things. Before long he had a fairly good picture of the area out front of the building. He felt confident that with the right rifle he could take out anything in front of him from where he sat. But he couldn't see it all.

Mark decided to make a return trip to the area in a couple of nights and set up behind the building. There he would duplicate his information gathering to detail out his plans. The fact that John had said many of the gang members had prior military and law enforcement experience was beginning to show. The theater was indeed a difficult location to hit.

Thirty minutes later he decided it would be

a good idea to head for the truck. He quietly packed up his scope and replaced the chair, then headed back toward the main floor and the rear exit.

He again scanned the church yard with the monocular and stepped outside, gently closing the door behind him. As he crossed the yard he became aware of the sound of voices approaching from his right. That was where he needed to go. Who would be up and about in this neighborhood at this time of day?

Mark slipped back behind the overgrown bushes at the corner of the church building a few seconds before a pair of heavily armed men stepped into view. He considered using the monocular again, but didn't want a sudden movement to draw their attention. Instead, he just stood by quietly and observed. His hand moved slowly to the grip of the 1911 as his eyes tracked their every move down the sidewalk. They stopped briefly in front of the church, their voices low enough that Mark couldn't discern their conversation.

One man lit a cigarette, illuminating his

face for a couple of seconds before handing the lighter back to his associate. In the dim glow of the flame, Mark could see that the man was Caucasian with a thin mustache and greasy hair partially obscured by a bandana. Over his shoulder was the barrel of a rifle, possibly an AR, but in the moment's opportunity Mark couldn't be sure. The other man's back was turned to Mark's position, so he couldn't get any useful information about him other than he also carried a rifle and it looked to be some type of AK.

Finally the pair moved on in the direction of the theater, their voices trailing off in the distance. Mark waited a few more minutes before stepping from his hiding place and silently working his way back to the truck.

From a distance he looked back toward the church and thought he saw movement along some of the other streets. Were they running patrols through the neighborhood? He needed to know, but didn't want to find out. Maybe he could determine more on his next recce.

Stealthily, Himes made his way through the

streets and back to the parking garage. As he stepped out of the elevator and onto the level where his truck waited, the sun was just beginning to break over the city. The timing was pretty good. Much longer on the streets and he might have been spotted by the patrols.

He opened the door on his truck and stuffed the bag in the passenger side. Something caught his eye on the street below. More movement. Was he being followed?

He removed his spotting scope from the truck and turned his attention back to the sidewalks, careful to make sure he didn't show what he was doing to the security cameras behind him. One was pointed away from him, back down the ramp toward street level, but another was aimed almost his direction. Though Himes wasn't even sure if it worked, there was no reason to raise suspicion by flaunting the optic around in plain sight.

There, on the sidewalk, alone, strode the visage of a young lady out for a morning jog. Her blonde ponytail bounced back and forth as she ran with an almost comedic look. From his angle he couldn't see her face clearly, but from what he did see she appeared to be in her mid to late twenties and was in very good condition. The tight fitting yoga shorts left very little to the imagination. She also wore a baggy grey tee shirt with something screen printed across the front, but Mark couldn't tell what it said. On her left arm was a pouch that held her music player and he could make out the headset that was pumping her workout music even from that distance.

He turned to put the scope back, thinking to himself how curious it was that someone like that would be jogging through this neighborhood. He had worried about appearing out of place, but this young lady really stood out. As he reached for the door handle, he heard something back on the street. It sounded like voices. He turned again and saw a vehicle had pulled alongside the girl and a pair of young men got out.

"Wait a minute," Mark mumbled to himself, "What's this?"

He swung the scope back up to his eye and wondered if he should grab the duffel bag. Despite his speed with assembling the AR, it was a very short barrel so it wouldn't be accurate at this distance. It would also be loud and he'd prefer the suppressor was attached to at least reduce the noise from the stubby barrel, but that meant more time to assemble it. Depending on what was going on down there, she may not have time to spare.

The men got on either side of her and were continually reaching for her. First one, then the other made aggressive advances toward the young woman as she was being backed into a small alleyway off to the right. Mark reached for the AR instinctively, wanting so badly to help, but unsure of what he could do from there.

Suddenly, the man on the girl's right lunged forward. She kicked him square in the crotch, dropping him to the ground as his partner moved in from her left. She turned to address him with a palm strike to the face before running into the alley.

"Bad move, girl," Mark said as he shifted his position and began to draw the compact rifle out. The first man was back on his feet and headed into the alley as well. Clearly he was more than a little irritated. Marked adjusted for a better view of what was going on, but from his position he just couldn't see down the alley. As he considered jumping in the truck to go and help he heard a distinctive, but quiet sound. Gunfire.

Two shots popped from the alley followed by shouting and another pair of shots. Mark eased the gun back into the bag and watched the alley for movement. He began to make mental notes of the vehicle and descriptions of the men so he could tell John. They may have just killed the girl, but they wouldn't get away with it. Not if he had anything to do with it.

A figure appeared at the entrance to the alley. Cautiously looking from left to right, the girl emerged from the passage. She tugged at her shirt tail, then turned and ran down the sidewalk, almost as if she were continuing her morning run, but at a considerably faster pace.

Mark watched as she drew closer to the garage, but she quickly made a left turn and disappeared behind some bushes and small trees that were enough to obscure her identity from him. He would give John a call and tell him what he could, but he already knew there wouldn't be enough to merit any investigation.

Chapter 7

Saturday finally arrived at the Himes home and Mark was delighted to fire up the grill. Soon the guests, John and Miranda, would be there. He had selected some choice items for their meal from the stockpile in the freezer; deer steaks, pork chops and pork loin courtesy of their neighbors down the road. Mark had suggested more than once that he and Angie consider raising a few hogs to supplement the groceries, but she had always stood firmly against it. As long as the Roberts family had the hogs she was satisfied that they didn't need any.

Before long John and Miranda were at the front door. Angie welcomed them inside and was surprised to receive a bouquet of flowers in return.

"These are lovely, but you really didn't need to go to any trouble."

"Oh, it wasn't any trouble at all, Mrs. Himes," Miranda said.

"It's Angie, please. I'm not old enough to claim 'Mrs. Himes' yet." Both ladies laughed and Angie led them into the family room.

"Mark is manning the grill. You are welcome to go out and make sure he's cooking things right. He doesn't like me critiquing his work, so I just stay out of the way and take care of everything else."

"I'll check on him," John replied, "He could probably use a little critiquing."

"Is there anything I can do, Angie?" Miranda asked as she stepped into the kitchen area.

"No, no. You're a guest here, Miranda. You go get comfortable and relax. That was the whole idea behind inviting you both here today. To get you away from all the phones and traffic so you could unwind a little."

Miranda pulled a chair up to the small breakfast table off to the side of the kitchen. From there she could carry on a conversation with Angie while still being able to see the back yard where John and Mark were.

"So," Angie began, "Mark tells me you have a little book store over on Fourth Avenue, is that right?"

"Yes. I opened it about three years ago after I left the IT career path."

"Wow. That's a big change, isn't it? From computer programming to selling books?"

"Yeah, I was getting pretty burned out at work. A lot of what I did was network security and that can get pretty frustrating. The whole security aspect is so fluid. It constantly changes and you really have to stay current on things to be effective. If you could see the future you'd do even better.

"Anyway, I have always been a reader. I told John and Mark I'm actually a huge nerd. I love books, and video games, and sci-fi, and everything else nerdy I can fit into my day."

Angie laughed at the thought of the attractive woman at her table trash talking other gamers.

"You know, when Ashley was still little, Mark and John both had game consoles. They would get online and play for hours sometimes. I thought I was going to have to throw the thing out more than once."

Miranda laughed and raised a hand with a shameful expression on her face, "Guilty here as well," she said.

"Andy and Ashley control the thing now. Of course, it isn't the same one Mark had years ago; he finally wore that one out, so he had to 'upgrade.' Now the kids can hand him his butt in pretty much any game we have. Funny how things come full circle like that, huh?" Angie smiled, "Oh, do you want anything to drink? I didn't mean to be rude. I'm so sorry."

"Oh, no, Angie, I'm fine. Really. I feel like I'm the one being rude by not helping out."

Angie stopped for a moment, then turned to Miranda, "Well, if you insist, I could use a little help getting the table set. Normally the kids do that for me, but they are both outside playing and I really don't feel like listening to them complain about me interrupting."

"Absolutely!" Miranda stood, "Where do I start?"

Further Reduction

Outside Mark and John were huddled around the grill discussing various other topics of importance.

"Man," John began, "I've never met anyone like her. She's incredible. I owe you big time for hooking us up."

Mark smiled as he flipped the steaks

"My pleasure. She is a very impressive girl. I have to be honest, though. I thought you might be a little intimidated by her IQ and independence. A lot of guys would be turned off by that."

"Oh, no. We were talking at dinner the other night and she confessed that a lot of guys she had gone out with were that way. They couldn't handle being the dumb one of the date. The way I look at it, it balances us out more. She's a lot smarter in some things than I am, like network stuff and classic literature, but I pull ahead on other things like law and tactics. We still have the middle ground that we are both comfortable with and that helps bridge the intellectual gaps."

John was smiling from ear to ear. Mark had never seen his friend so enthralled with anyone before.

"Hey, if you're happy, I'm happy. I gotta ask, though, what's her baggage?"

John shot a puzzled look at Mark.

"You know," Mark continued, "There's got to be something. Some little thing that hasn't shown yet because the relationship is fresh. Like Angie; who would have guessed that she can snore like a freight train?"

John hadn't thought about it before. He glanced back at the house and his mind began to race. What if she had some really annoying habits? What if she had a checkered past? For that matter, what if she was outright crazy and this was all for show?

"Dude," Mark snapped at his friend, "I'm just messing with you. She's great. Don't worry about it. Now make yourself useful and hand me that platter. It's time to eat."

John smiled back at his friend as he reached for the platter. Of course Mark was just messing around. There couldn't be any baggage about Miranda. She was perfect.

Mark called the kids in and they all made their way to the table. Miranda was setting the last of the plates down as they all shuffled in. Angie explained the process of how the meal would be like a self-serve buffet and seating was around the main table. The last comment was directed more toward the children, who preferred to eat in front of the television.

During the course of the meal Mark and John brought Miranda up to speed on their respective antics over the years of their friendship. Some were a little more embarrassing than others, but all were in good fun.

Miranda, in turn, told of some of her own pranks and situations during her years in IT.

"We used to have cubicle warfare," she said, "Everyone in the office was constantly doing something to someone else for a laugh. We had this one manager who was totally tech ignorant. He was too easy a target to pass up.

"The guy was arrogant and snooty so he always talked down to everyone. Anyway, Tim, one of the other security guys, brought in this little circuit board one day. It was about the size of a half-dollar and all it did was make a simple beep. It sounded a lot like an error beep on a PC, you know?

"Well, Tim goes to this guy's office while he's in a meeting and hides this thing somewhere in the room. We didn't go with him, so the only one who knew where it was was Tim. After the meeting the manager returns to his office and within an hour he's on the phone with the IT manager complaining about the beeping.

"Our manager didn't know anything about it, so he played it off and let it go. By the end of the day, this poor idiot has almost torn his office apart trying to find the source of the beep. He had us in there disassembling his PC and swapping printers, but nothing he did helped. It was the hardest thing in the world not to laugh at the guy while we were taking his system out."

"Oh, man! That's great!" John laughed, "Did anyone ever find it?"

"No. Tim finally slipped back into the office one day and pulled it out, but he never said where he put it and nobody ever found it. That thing was in there for about two weeks."

"So the manager went crazy for two weeks before you guys finally let him off the hook?" Angie's jaw dropped.

"No. We found out later that he took some vacation time to 'calm his nerves' the second week. That was when Tim decided not to waste the battery on an empty room."

"Man, I could cause so much trouble with that," John said, "The Chief is about as technologically challenged as they come. That would drive him nuts in a matter of minutes!"

"I think Tim got it from a website called Think Geek. I want to say it was an Annoy-a-tron, or something. Loads of fun for the nerd in everyone." Miranda laughed.

"Just remember the Chief carries a gun," Mark popped back at John.

After dinner the kids helped put the plates away and clear the table while Angie and Mark loaded the dishwasher. Soon they all gathered in the living room and the youngsters asked of they could play video games.

Angie cut a glance over at Miranda, who was already starting to smile.

"I have an idea," Angie said, "Why don't we let Miranda and John play too?"

"Okay," Ashley said without a second thought.

Andy selected a multiplayer first person shooter from the cabinet, then turned to his sister, "Kids against grown ups?" Both of them smiled.

"Uh oh," Mark said, "They're setting you guys up. Better watch them."

Miranda laughed, "I think we'll be alright. But, I may be a little rusty." She laughed and leaned on John's arm as Ashley handed them controllers.

When the game booted up John smiled at Mark, "Man, remember when we used to stay up playing online years ago? That was so much fun! I used to beat you down all the time!"

"I always got you back, though. Usually from a distance and usually pretty quickly. If *someone* didn't camp at all the spawn points you never would have scored a point on me."

All the while Miranda was listening and learning about how the boys used to play. She knew that their methods would probably be the same now as they were then.

During the first game, Miranda played casually, letting her opponents win time after time, learning their techniques and their favorite moves. She also watched John's screen when she was waiting to be back in the game. Learning his playing style was as important as learning the kids'.

During the second game, she dialed it up a bit, respectably taking second place of the four. During the third game, however, she unleashed her skills and dominated the game. The kids were awestruck as the newcomer took them each out, one by one, then turned on John and hunted him down as well.

"Hey!" he cried, "We're on the same team!"

She laughed out loud as she blurted, "Tag! You're it!"

"Every player for themselves!" cried Ashley and with that, the next few games were four way melees.

Miranda graciously let the kids win a few times, but was unrelenting toward John. Occasionally, he would get an advantage, but it was rare, so she let him enjoy it. Payback was usually swift and sure unless she wanted to build the anticipation and found a nice hiding place somewhere on the map. There she would sit and watch until the time was right to jump back in the action.

Ashley and Andy were having the time of their lives, but it all had to come to a close. It was getting late and their guests still had to get home. Besides, they might have wanted a little time to themselves.

"Can they come over again and play?" Andy asked with a massive grin across his face.

"Yeah, can they?" Ashley was just as excited.

"Well, that's up to Miranda and John. They are always welcome," Angie replied, "I think you have made some new friends, Miranda."

She smiled back at the kids with a sparkle

in her eyes, "Oh, I'll be back. I owe Andy for that rocket launcher kill earlier."

Andy grinned a bashful grin.

"Yeah, you thought I forgot about that, didn't you?" She laughed, "Next time I'm bringing pizza. No need for your mom and dad to have to cook. They can join in on the gaming. Deal?"

"Deal!" they both shouted in unison.

John and Miranda said their goodbyes and headed for the car. As Mark closed the front door he watched the tail lights disappear down the road.

"Okay guys, bedtime," he said, turning off the front porch light, "You know the drill."

As the pair made their way to their rooms Angie and Mark couldn't help but laugh at how they carried on about Miranda's gaming skills.

"Well, I think she made a good impression on the kids. What do you think?"

"I'm not sure," Mark replied sarcastically, "I think they're just excited to get pizza."

"Yeah," she continued with a giggle, "You're probably right."

Mark began putting the controllers away

and Angie tidied up the living room a bit. When they were done they both flopped on the couch.

"I hope those two work out," Angie sighed, "She seems like a great match for him. And John has needed something in his life besides work for a long time."

"Me too. I know John is completely head over heels for her. She seems to be the same for him. Still, the relationship is young. A lot of things can happen." Mark leaned back and dropped his arm around his wife.

"Don't you jinx this, Mark Himes."

"I'm not jinxing anything," Mark said, "I'm just saying there are a lot of things they still have to learn about each other and, well, you know things can happen. I'm just being realistic."

Angie glanced at the clock on the wall.

"Well, come on, Mr. Realist. It's bedtime for the big kids too."

Chapter 8

Mark crept back into the neighborhood around the back side of the theater under the blanket of pre-dawn darkness. Again, he carried his 1911 and the short AR in an SBR configuration. He had skipped packing one extra magazine for the AR to allow room for a suppressor for his 1911. Following the close call last time, he felt like it might be wiser to opt for extra stealth over extra firepower.

Moving from yard to yard, sweeping the areas he crossed with a quick glance through the night vision monocular, he made very good time to the old school building that was his objective. A heavy dew was on the ground, so he was concerned about leaving footprints on the concrete of any sidewalks he crossed. Maybe he would be lucky and the patrols wouldn't notice any prints he might leave. Maybe he would be luckier still and they would think they were their own. In either case, he stayed to the grass as much as possible.

Soon he had arrived at the school, an imposing structure built in the 1930's before consideration was given to handicapped ramps or wheelchair access. The gym sat to the right of the front door, above the cafeteria, and the library above that. The entirety of the left side of the facility was classrooms and office space. Out back was a small addition that housed the vocational shops and classrooms.

The cafeteria was partially below ground level, which offered Mark no opportunities to observe, or shoot from. That was unfortunate because it did offer the easiest ingress and egress. His best vantage would be the upper floors, and he quickly made for them, working as quietly and cautiously as possible in the gloomy darkness.

The monocular was to his eye almost all the time as he inched rapidly through the lower floor and to the stairs. The green image through the low light device swept across the hallways and into the recesses of each room as he passed. Amazingly, he was the only thing moving through the structure aside from the rather large rodents he stirred from time to time.

He reached the upper floor library and scanned the large windows for a good observation point, finally settling on the corner nearest the hallway leading into the classroom section of the building. The hallway offered a better angle, but it had glass on the front and back, so there was an increased chance of being spotted from behind by someone outside the building.

He quietly set his spotting scope and notepad out and found an old chair in the corner to use as well. The sun would be up in about two and a half hours, so he worked at a steady pace. Soon he could spy the theater in the distance, some 650 yards away.

The rear of the building was much easier to observe thanks to additional lighting around the area. With the sloping roofline, Mark could also see the entire top of the building. What he saw sent a cold chill down his spine.

On the roof, obscured from view his first night, he could clearly see a pair of what appeared to be machine gun nests or observation posts. There were armed guards patrolling the front and rear of the roof, with two small covered shacks surrounded by low walls of what looked like sandbags for protection from the elements as well as returning gunfire from below.

The only windows on the entire building were on the front. That was only logical given the original purpose, but that made his only opportunity for a shot the rear entrance. There were a number of vehicles parked around back, some actually very nice, but then there were other curious models in the mix. One was a four wheel drive truck with a heavy roll bar and an unusual seat mounted to the bed floor. Another was a large box van. Mark could tell from the way the rear end was squatted that it was over the design limit for the vehicle. Either it was full of some heavy stuff, or the vehicle had been up-armored and weighed an extra ton or two. Mark noted anything he saw and the pages were beginning to fill up.

He also tried to watch the people on the roof and those coming and going below. If there was any formality to the group, there should be a schedule for patrols. If he could figure that out, he might be able to better figure on an opportunity to take his target out.

The back door opened and light spilled across the parking area, silhouetting four individuals for just a moment. From his position, he couldn't see into the building, but he checked his time and noted the people in his book. Two males and what appeared to be two females. All armed with at least handguns. One of the males was carrying a pump shotgun over his left shoulder, possibly a Mossberg. The other man carried a rifle but Himes couldn't tell make or model. It looked like a bolt action, but the way the man held it he couldn't be sure.

One woman had a pair of pistols tucked in the waistband of her jeans, well, what was left of her jeans. They were torn up and down both legs on the front as if they had been rescued from the ravages of an angry lawnmower. Well, that was the style and Mark supposed it would be in poor taste to go on patrol and not be fashionable.

The fourth individual was an enigma. Himes assumed it was a woman by the way she stood and moved, but the clothes and hair suggested she was male. In the early morning darkness, over the distance, he couldn't be positive. Beside the note of her description he jotted the word 'female' with a question mark in parentheses. She carried a single pistol in a holster on her right side. As they stood talking she slipped a jacket on and turned to walk away. The other woman followed soon after. The men headed the opposite direction and soon all four were in the shadows.

Soon after their departure two more figures stepped into the doorway from the shadowy night and were swallowed by the building. Mark checked his watch; 4:00 a.m. Perhaps that was the shift change for the patrols.

He scanned the exterior of the building up near the roof line. There, on each corner, he could see a small security camera. From time to time the one on the right side would actually point enough of his direction that he could see the tiny red LED indicating the power was on.

He needed to see if there were any other people on the street and how frequently the patrols rotated in and out. He debated staying in the building all day and observing the activity, but he wasn't prepared to do that. He hadn't expected to see what he saw. Maybe he would come back a little earlier in the evening and stake it out with some food and coffee. Coffee. The thought made him smile broadly to himself.

He took a look at his watch and realized he needed to be packing and on the move.

"*One last look and I'm gone,*" he thought to himself.

As he leaned into the spotting scope he thought, just for a second, that the cameras had stopped moving. He focused on the one with the bright LED and it was still sweeping the area out back. Mark began to pack his gear and move quietly from his perch toward the stairs.

As he got to the top of the steps he heard movement below.

"*Uh oh,*" he thought, "*Company's coming.*"

He slipped back up the steps to the library

level and moved as quickly and quietly as possible into the classroom side of the complex as he could without risking being spotted through the windows.

Confident that he had made it without being noticed, he moved around a corner and into a classroom. He waited for just a few seconds, listening to the ambient noises for any sounds of movement that might be heading his way. As he stood, he carefully slid his hand back into the pouch of the duffel bag, carefully peeling apart the Velcro strips to retrieve the suppressor he had packed for the 1911. Before leaving home he had decided to "wet" it to be on the safe side. A couple of CC's of some wire pulling grease from the hardware store injected into the baffles would make the pistol almost as quiet as Hollywood would have you think they really were.

Moments later he had the device threaded on the barrel and stood ready to pick between fight or flight. He preferred flight, but wasn't sure how many people were outside or where they were. It could be a single individual looking for a place to sleep or it could be a patrol of two or more checking the building for security risks, like him. Himes slowly slid the bag from his back to his chest in the hopes that the extra layers of Kevlar and padding might offer some protection should he need it.

A garbled voice echoed up the stairway as a radio came to life. The voice that responded was female; probably one of the two that he had seen earlier. She spoke in a low voice, so her words were unintelligible. By the sounds, she was alone and probably close to his seat by the window and heading his way. Soon he could see the beam of a flashlight sweeping the hallway from side to side. She was on her way and covering ground quickly.

Mark moved silently back away from the door and hugged the wall tightly. He extended the pistol along the wall and aimed at about chest height. If anyone stepped through the doorway, he should be able to drop them with a single shot.

A few seconds later and the footsteps were right outside the door. He watched as the flashlight beam pierced the darkness of the room and swept left to right, illuminating the wall opposite of him. She hardly slowed down. Within moments she was down the steps and gone. Mark silently exhaled a huge breath he'd been holding for what seemed like an eternity. He held his position for a few more minutes and then slowly picked his way out of the room and back through the library to the stairs. That would put him closer to the cafeteria and his easiest way out.

Finally he stepped through the cafeteria doorway at the bottom of the gym steps and eyed the back door directly across from him.

"Well, I thought Joe was just messing with me," the woman said.

Mark's blood turned cold as he looked to his right and saw the manly looking woman standing there in the darkness.

"What you doin' in here? You don't look homeless to me. Lookin' for trouble?" She stepped closer to Mark, sizing him up with a peculiar interest in the large bag on his shoulder.

"What you got in that bag, man? Maybe I'll let you go and not say nuthin' if it's somethin' good."

Mark kept silent, slowly turning himself in her direction but keeping the 1911 from her view.

"Then again, maybe I'll just slit your throat and take it myself."

Mark glanced down and saw that the woman had a large folding knife in her right hand. The pistol was still neatly tucked in its holster. He smiled a dirty smile.

"Now, I don't want any trouble, ma'am," Mark began, "I'm just looking at the building."

"You some kind of real estate man? Think you gonna buy this and turn it into Trump Tower or somethin'?" the woman sneered, almost laughing at her own comment, "Gimme the bag. Now."

Mark reached for the shoulder strap and gripped it as if he were about to drop it on the ground at her feet.

In a single, fluid motion, he turned and slung the bag onto his chest while bringing the pistol up from behind it. She lunged at him, knife in hand, not realizing she had practically impaled herself on the business end of the .45. Mark pressed the trigger twice and a muffled cough spat two 185 grain hollow points into her chest cavity. The sound of the brief struggle almost totally concealed the sound of the gunfire.

A look of shock poured over the woman's face as she plunged the knife into the bag, the blade deflecting off the magazines and suppressor that remained in the secret pouch. Mark twisted the grip of the pistol, pointing the barrel upward, toward her head and driving it deeper into her chest as he squeezed a third and final shot off.

She gripped his shoulder tightly and the look of shock became an expression of fear as she slumped to the floor.

Mark's mind raced with a flurry of thoughts. That sounded a lot louder than it should. Did anyone hear? Should he move her body? Should he take her weapon or radio? Where was her partner? Was the school going to be watched more closely now? Where else could he take a shot from? Suddenly he became aware of his situation and location and decided that he needed to get out of the building. Her sidekick obviously hadn't heard the shots or she would have been there by now. None of the other patrols were close enough to respond either. He quickly grabbed his burn phone and snapped a picture of the body that laid at his feet. He would send it to John once he got to a more secure location and see who she was. For now, it was time to move.

Chapter 9

As Himes made for the truck he kept thinking how he wished he had taken the woman's radio. If he had he could monitor the traffic and possibly tell where the other patrols were and if they had found her yet. Then again, if they noticed the radio missing, it might be a red flag that could result in heavier patrols or even occupation of the building. Plus they would, no doubt, change any communications plans they had in place. Frequencies, code words, call signs; they would probably all change, making monitoring useless if they had plans to start with, of course. Seeing how organized they appeared, Mark was sure they did.

He cut across a number of yards, sweeping in a wide arc around the neighborhood, following his path in. Scanning the houses and yards with the night vision monocular quickly before moving through was second nature, but his adrenaline was still pumping, making him rush.

"Be quick, but don't be careless," Himes thought to himself.

He rounded the corner of a small house with a neatly kept yard and a valiant attempt at landscaping. He had cut through here on the way in a couple of hours earlier. The residence looked almost out of place in the neighborhood except for the worn path across the corner of the yard. Apparently the neighborhood watch didn't mind cutting through to do their patrols.

He quickly swept the yard with his eye pressed into the cup of the optic and stepped around into the back yard. After only a few steps he realized he had made a mistake.

"You might want to change shoes next time," the voice was loud enough to hear, but quiet enough that it didn't carry far.

Mark jumped; startled to find that he had been spotted by someone and that someone was very close. He swung around with the monocular and saw a hefty elderly black man on the back porch of the house. A large unlit cigar dangled in his right hand. Mark had the 1911 up and pointed in the man's direction, but the man made no aggressive moves. He just cocked his head with a curious expression.

"How many rounds are you carrying?" He asked.

"What?" Mark was confused at the question.

"In your pouch. How many magazines are you carrying? I heard them rattle when you jumped."

Mark lowered the pistol and stared at the enigmatic man.

"If you plan on fighting a war, you'd better have enough ammo, son."

"How did you…"

"I might not be able to see, but I can hear a gnat fart on top of that old school building down there. Like I heard some gunfire from that direction earlier. Quiet. Suppressed. That you?"

Mark stood silently. Desperately he tried to assess the situation.

"Yeah. That was me. Self defense. I…"

"Don't doubt it for a second, son. There's

some bad folks around here. A man's gotta be careful where he goes and when he goes there.

"But, there's a lot of good folks around here too. Folks who just want to live their lives and die of old age."

Mark swallowed hard before asking, "So, are you a good guy or a bad guy?"

The man smiled broadly, "I've been both. These days I like it quiet. I just want to enjoy my yard and my cigars. I got all my fighting urges out a long time ago. Little place called Vietnam. You may have heard of it."

Mark smiled, "Well, thank you for your service, sir. I appreciate it," Himes glanced around the neighborhood nervously, "I, uh, I really need to be going."

"Hmph," the man started, "Yeah, a white dude like you kind of sticks out around here. Others might not notice it, but you smell too clean to be one of them," he gestured with a nod toward the theater.

"I thought you were blind," Mark said, somewhat surprised at the man's comments.

"I am, legally. Can't see beyond a few inches worth a damn. But you sound white. You smell white. You're in this neighborhood early in the morning with a bag of ammo, which means you're carrying a weapon to use it in. I'm going to go out on a limb and say it's an AR-15 or an M-4. The magazines clattered like a pair of fully loaded ones. Something else in there with them. Probably the suppressor for that .45 you've got. Am I right?"

Mark stood there speechless. For a blind man, he was deadly accurate on perception. He didn't know if he should answer or not, fearing the man might be setting him up somehow, but he couldn't tell. Giving nothing away was the best option he had, wasn't it? Still, there was something about the man's tone. He wasn't raising his voice to alert anyone. He could have probably gotten a patrol here by now, if that had been his intent.

"You're not a very talkative fellow, are you? Well, I suppose it really ain't my business, is it? I would like to know one thing, though," The man shifted his weight in the aluminum framed patio chair.

"What would that be, sir?"

He sat forward slightly, as if about to divulge a secret of monumental proportions.

"Are you doing the right thing?"

Mark studied the man's face as best he could in the dimness of the early morning hours and considered the gravity of the question.

"I sure hope so, sir."

"Then Godspeed to you. And don't call me sir. I never made more than corporal."

Himes turned to leave, then stopped and asked, "A question, corporal?"

The old man smiled, "Yes?"

"You weren't out here when I came in. Why are you out here now? Did you hear me the first time?"

The man chuckled quietly.

"Son, I haven't slept well since 1967. I also have a wife that despises my cigars. Every morning, before the sun comes up or my wife rolls out, I sneak outside with the Dutch Masters for a few minutes. It doesn't matter much if I turn the lights on or not, so you wouldn't have known I was up when you came through the first time. I heard your squeaky shoes as you trucked through by the begonias. That's an unfortunate side effect of wearing rubber soled shoes on wet grass."

Mark smiled. The man was sharp, he had to admit.

"Go on, now. My wife will be up in a bit and if she sees you out here she'll invite you in for breakfast instead of taking me to the buffet at Pancake Country. She's a terrible cook."

"Consider me gone, corporal," Himes smiled, "Take care of yourself."

"You too, son."

With that Mark slipped silently across the man's yard and off into the darkness. He made a hasty pathway to the truck only ducking into the shadows a couple of times as patrols passed. They were in a rush, so he assumed his mess had been discovered in the cafeteria. The sooner he was at the truck, the safer he would be.

Finally, after an eternity of dark streets and alleys he was at the ground floor of the garage.

Soon he was in the elevator and on the way up. His mind raced with all the things he had encountered that night. There seemed to be no good approach to the situation.

The building might as well be a bank vault. No windows or doors to allow him adequate visibility inside, armed guards all around the neighborhood, firing positions on the roof, what looked like armored vehicles out back. It would be easier trying to rob Fort Knox than getting this target.

Mark stepped out of the elevator and quietly but quickly made it to the truck. Soon he was on the way home.

After a couple of hours of much needed sleep, Mark contacted John to update him on the job. He sent a simple text message from his burn phone saying, "Situation complicated. Contact me."

While he waited for John's response he busied himself with the search for the vigilante. Perhaps stepping away from the job would offer some clarity the next time he looked at it. Sometimes a fresh perspective is what you have to have.

He pulled up a digital map of the city with red dots superimposed at all the known locations where the killings had taken place. The end result of his plotting and tracking looked almost identical to the map on Dahlgren's wall.

Himes applied a new layer to the image, one that he could draw on without fear of disturbing what he already had, and discard if needed. It was the digital equivalent of laying a sheet of tracing paper on a physical map to sketch ideas out, but it was all on the computer.

On the new layer he began to draw a series of lines in a messy connect the dots fashion, trying to link each location to the others. He hoped that there would be a common point of intersection among them, establishing a 'ground zero' so to speak.

After several renditions of this technique there was nothing to work from. Yes, the points did intersect, but not at any one particular location. There didn't seem to be any underlying logic to it.

He deleted the layer and started with a fresh one, this time focusing on smaller slices of the larger picture.

Rather than tying all the points on the map together, he focused on smaller clusters of activity. A pair of incidents connected in the southern part of the city, then the ones in the western area, and so forth. Nothing seemed to tie the clusters together either. There were no common landmarks or features to associate one with another.

Out of frustration, Mark began drawing lines from one cluster to another. When he did that, the clusters all converged in a single, general area. It was a large area, but it was a possibility. He decided it may be time for an up close look at the region, just to see if there was any reasonable basis to pursue it.

He printed off a copy of the map and began to gather his gear up when his phone rang. It was John.

"Hey, man. What's up?"

"Any chance you'd have time to meet this morning?"

"Sure. When and where?"

"I'm about to head into town and check out a location that might be a starting point for the vigilante search. It's a shot in the dark, but at least it's a shot. I'll meet you at the gas station at Kimball and Barron in, say, an hour. Will that work?"

"I'll be there."

"Oh, speaking of shots in the dark, I need to show you a picture too. It's been an interesting day already."

Mark pulled into the parking lot at the gas station just as John parked his unmarked car and stepped out. Himes pulled alongside the cruiser and gestured for his friend to get in. John motioned to the store, and then held up a finger to indicate he was going inside first.

Mark shut off the engine and waited with his map in his hands. Within a few minutes Thompson appeared at the passenger side door with a drink and candy bar.

"You didn't get me anything?"

John laughed, "You've got legs. Go get something."

He seated himself in the truck and glanced at the map in Mark's possession.

"What's this? You turning into the Chief on me?"

"Huh?"

"Dahlgren has a map almost identical to that one on the wall of his office. He's been tracking crimes all over the city with it. He's not as tech savvy as you." A sarcastic smile stretched across Thompson's face.

"Well, I wouldn't say I'm savvy, but I know enough to be dangerous."

"That, you do."

Mark smiled at the double meaning behind John's comment.

"This is a plot of all the vigilante strikes you told me about. There doesn't seem to be anything connecting them. I tried to connect the dots, but they converge in a couple of different spots, so…"

"So you couldn't establish a home base for him. Yeah, we've done that as well.," John replied.

"Well, then I did this with the clusters. If

you take the clusters and connect them, instead of the individual hits, you can establish a general common area. What do you think?"

John studied the map for a minute.

"That's a big area, man. I mean, it's smaller than the whole city, but you're still talking about several city blocks each way. Do you think this is the way to go?"

"I don't know. All I know right now is that I'm tired of trying to figure out how to hit that stupid theater and I need another outlet for my frustrations."

John looked the map over again.

"Miranda's apartment is over here. She's just outside the edge of your focal point."

Mark looked over at the map, "I didn't know that. That's a pretty nice part of town. Can she afford that on bookstore pay?

"I was at her place last night for dinner. It's a really impressive apartment. Great view of downtown, very spacious. Almost looked like it was torn from a magazine. As for the cost, well, mom and dad are doing well, like *very* well, and she has IT contracts that pay pretty nicely too. She isn't hurting for cash."

"So, how are things going with you two? She isn't tired of you yet?"

John smiled, "Not yet. They say absence makes the heart grow fonder and I guess that might be the key. Between our schedules, we don't see each other but a few times a week. She mentioned that she'd love for me to meet her family. I don't know if I'm up for that yet or not."

"Wait, you're afraid to commit to a young, attractive, successful woman whose family is loaded and has a huge ranch out west? Are you stupid?"

John laughed, "No, I'm just not sure we're to a 'commitment' point yet. I just don't want to rush anything. Like you said, she might be outright crazy. I don't want to tie the knot and then find that out.

"Oh," John said, changing the subject before Mark could press any harder, "You said you were getting frustrated with the theater. Did something happen?"

Mark pulled his phone out and showed him the photograph of the woman in the cafeteria.

"She snuck in on me while I was sneaking out this morning; tried to gut me with that knife beside her hand. Look at the gear."

John studied the image, "So, they are well equipped. Looks like they're using radios to manage the patrols and probably general comms. Did you take hers?"

"No," Mark replied, "I thought about it, but I figured if I did they would probably have a backup communications plan and it wouldn't help anything."

"Yeah, that's probably right. If they are organized I'm guessing they would. That radio looks kind of like the ones we issue to our officers. Not exactly, but I wouldn't be surprised if they couldn't hear us. It would be to their advantage."

Mark started to mention the corporal and their encounter, but decided to not bother with it. No need to complicate things any more than they already were. Besides, if John thought the job was compromised, he might pull the plug.

"Better still, they have what looked to be machinegun nests on top and possibly armored vehicles out back. They aren't like repurposed armored cars, but I think they may have some box vans that have been reinforced. They squat lower to the ground than they should in the back. Of course, they may just be really full of heavy cargo, but I couldn't see inside to be sure."

"Are you kidding me? Machinegun nests on the roof?" John's eyes grew large and his mouth dropped a little.

"I didn't see any machineguns, but I did see a pair of firing or observation positions on the roof. One was at the front and one was at the rear. They had simple roofs over them and either sandbag or concrete bag walls stacked around."

John thought about all the information Mark had fed him on the location. He was beginning to get very concerned.

"Do you want to back off and call in SWAT to just raid and take them out?"

"From what I've seen there, I think SWAT may be outgunned. And if these guys are eavesdropping on your comms, they'll know you're coming anyway. Let me work on it some more. There has to be a way."

"Okay," John sighed, "In the meantime I have something else to get your mind wrapped around, if you want it."

"Yeah, let me take a look. I need a mental vacation from these two for a little bit."

"Be right back," John said as he slipped out of the truck.

He reached into the cruiser and grabbed a small packet, then swiftly got back into the pickup.

"Here you go. We've tried to keep this out of the news as much as we could. We're hoping to catch the guy before he sees his name in lights. We don't want him to get famous before we can get him stopped."

Mark opened the envelope and pulled out a stack of pages. Inside were photographs and reports about a series of sexual assaults. Different victims, but they all described the same attacker. At the bottom of the stack was a sketch of the assailant.

"Nice looking fellow," Mark commented, the sarcasm clear in his tone.

"Yeah, he's a real winner. He seems to favor the area around Carson Park a lot. We've stepped up patrols in that area to try and catch him, but haven't had any luck yet. So far he's attacked three women there. We haven't connected him to any other attacks, but we suspect there are others."

"Well," Mark said, looking up to the sky, "It looks like a lovely day for a stroll in the park. Right after I roll through this area." He pointed to the map where all the lines converged.

"Happy hunting, man. Let me know if I can help."

Chapter 10

Mark drove through the grid indicated on his map, trying to get a feel for the neighborhoods. It was largely a residential area, with a few businesses sprinkled throughout. In his old pickup truck, he looked a bit out of place. The luxurious homes sheltered multiple Mercedes and BMW vehicles in every carport or garage he saw. There was actually a limo parked out front of one with the driver by the rear doors.

"It must be nice," Mark sighed under his breath, "I'll never know."

He crisscrossed the area twice before settling on the idea that this part of town was too affluent to house any vigilantes he might be looking for. If there were a real-life Batman around, he couldn't see a cave entrance anywhere.

Himes mentally scrapped the idea of this as ground zero and turned toward Carson Park. Traffic was terrible and it took him longer to get there than he had expected. Mark hadn't been accustomed to driving in city traffic for a while, but he managed to reach his destination without issue.

When he strolled into the park he passed a small kiosk maintained by the Parks and Recreation Department. It housed a healthy sample of maps of the area highlighting items of interest for visitors. It wasn't exactly a proper piece of cartography, with some of the points of interest exaggerated like caricatures, but it would suffice. He grabbed a map and entered the park.

Carson Park was a bit of an enigma; it straddled the physical boundary between the older, more neglected part of town and the newer developments. On the west side of the park sat dilapidated storefronts and multi-story apartments that dated back to the 1920's and even older. On the east side were gleaming new high rise apartments, bars, restaurants, office buildings and stately structures in an array of sizes and shapes. The old buildings stood almost as if in defiance of change, but when you stood in the park, there in the midst of it all, you got the feeling that it was only a matter of time before they, like the time they were new, would soon be history.

Mark strolled about the winding pathways and across the lush green lawns of the commons for almost two hours, making notes in his notepad and marks on his map of possible hides as well as potential areas to catch his man. There was an abundance of shady alcoves and bushy areas that were difficult to see from the pathways. Add to that a number of large culverts and even tunnels that crossed under pedestrian bridges that could, in the absence of a large amount of visitors, be an easy place for him to strike. Mark decided he would contact John for additional details about the locations in each attack and note them along with his own findings to see if there was a pattern or at least a starting point. That would have to wait for a while. At the moment he had to swing by Deever's body shop for some supplies.

When Mark arrived at his workshop he immediately set about sorting his body shop booty into useful piles. Resins, fiberglass matt, chip brushes and other items soon piled in a corner while some fresh panels of Kevlar found their way onto his work bench. He hadn't looked at the damage from the knife attack yet, but he knew he was going to have to at least do some minor repair work to the duffel bag. It always struck him as odd that a material tough enough to stop a bullet would simply slice right away with a good knife.

He brought up the CAD program and opened up the file he had been working on for the previous several days. There, on the screen was a complicated assembly comprising a rifle receiver, barrel, magazine, and a bullpup stock that carried it all. The stock was designed with a separate section at the front that surrounded the barrel. A large cavity was left open so the barrel could "float" for accuracy and accommodate one of his custom suppressors.

He turned the layers off that contained the rifle components and the remaining assembly revealed a perfectly fitting stock to hold them all in position. Himes set about slicing the stock design into smaller chunks and saving each as a 3-D printable file format.

Soon he was submitting each chunk to the 3-D printer and slowly each section took shape. The printer did an excellent job of replicating the design, but was terribly slow. Each section could take hours to print, but Mark had little choice. The build volume of the printer was too small to print the whole stock at once. Still, it was cheaper than making it out of metal and easier than trying to fabricate out of wood. Besides, when it was assembled, there would be very little cleanup and tool work before he could get to making the mold.

It took a couple of days to get all the parts printed, but when they were finished he began to assemble them into the right and left halves of the stock. Patience, glue, and time were all factors. Once he had each half built he quickly checked them for fit with the receiver he had. Everything looked good. A little polish here and there and some sanding, actually lots of sanding, and he could move on to the next step.

He pulled the barrel out of storage and laid it across the table where he assembled a curious looking block onto the breach end. Mark had studied numerous designs for quick change barrel systems by a number of manufacturers. Ruger utilized a very effective design on their 10-22 break down models, but it was a small caliber. He feared it might not stand up to the power of a .308 round.

Many of the heavy machineguns used by militaries the world over used a quick change barrel system because the barrels would overheat during sustained fire. They could take the pressure, but weren't designed for the accuracy he would need.

His AR fell somewhere in the middle and that was where he began. Where he finished was a totally new design that allowed him to twist and unlock the barrel in about 1.5 seconds and to reassemble it in less than 3 seconds. The barrel locked in tightly enough that he could hold zero through the Leupold scope very well despite the optic being mounted off the barrel.

Assembling the barrel to the receiver and then putting both elements inside the prototype stock required a little finesse, but he finally got it worked out. A few tight spots had to be sanded some more and a couple of other areas relieved a bit, but it worked. He had allowed a generous amount of room for the quick change adapter, and it worked surprisingly well. Unfortunately, Himes had no idea how the complete rifle would work since the original stock didn't allow for the adapter and he didn't think it wise to modify it, just in case he had to resell the rifle one day in the original configuration. He would have to assemble and test fire it all within the new stock. That was the one thing he dreaded; test firing. He had always been careful with his designs and had never had any issues as far as safety went, but there was always the chance something could go wrong.

On the far end of the work bench sat a small frame, deep enough to hold the entire prototype stock. Mark mixed a healthy batch of silicone molding rubber and began to cast the molds for the stock. Once the stock was prepped and a coating of release agent applied, he began to cover the halves with a liberal amount of rubber. After several layers he could begin applying the fiberglass mother mold, which would provide stiffness and support to the otherwise flexible silicone.

The process, like the printing and assembly, was slow and tedious, but Mark knew if he rushed it would be a waste of time and money.

The following day he began to lay the fiberglass into the mold. Most of the morning was spent with a respirator on his face and a fan in the doorway trying to ventilate the shop. He tried to follow Rob Deevers' instructions as closely as he could, but he worried that he would forget something. Working with the resins was a time sensitive process, like the rubber before, but still, he tried to work carefully.

It would be the next day before he would remove the casting from the mold to allow plenty of curing time.

As soon as Angie and the kids had left for the day, Mark went to the shop and removed the mother molds from the silicone. He flipped the left half over and peeled the silicone off, revealing a pristine copy of the prototype stock. There was a little flash to trim and some sanding to do, but otherwise it looked incredibly good. He followed the same steps for the right half and test fit the two together.

Satisfied that it would work, he began to clean and prep for painting and final assembly. Once the cleanup was done on all the inside areas, he dry fit the receiver and barrel into the new design. It was like a big rigid glove. The smile on Mark's face couldn't be restrained.

He quickly set to work on the final sanding and priming for paint. He hoped that by the afternoon he could assemble and test fire it.

While the first coat of paint was drying, Mark tucked the molds away high on a shelf. He turned back to his work in time to see John standing in the doorway with a hand raised to knock.

"Hey, man. Come on in. What brings you around this time of day?"

"I didn't want to drop in unannounced, but I knew you said you were working on your stock so I figured you'd be out here. I tried to call, but you wouldn't answer your phone. Either of them, actually."

Mark realized he had been so anxious to finish the prototype that he left both phones in the house. Habitually he patted his pockets, even though he already knew what he'd done with them.

"Yeah, I left them inside. Sorry about that." He busied himself with cleaning up the rest of the mess left by the stock building process, "What's up?"

"Oh, I was on my way to pick up Miranda and had some information to give you, so I thought I'd swing by while I was out."

"Just 'in the neighborhood,' huh?" Mark smiled at his friend mockingly. Himes lived several miles outside the city limits, so there was no way he was just randomly passing by.

"Well, something like that, yeah," John smiled back, "I was going to touch base with you on the job situation. Have you had any luck anywhere? I know you have been stressing about them."

"Nope. Not a clue. I haven't figured out anything on how to get the theater job done without him poking his head out. He has no set schedule and I can't get inside either.

"Your vigilante is about as bad. I have no starting point. I checked out the area where all the clusters converge and it just doesn't look or feel right. People in that part of town wouldn't risk what they have to be any kind of avenging angel.

"I overlaid the points you gave me on the map of the park I had for the rapist job and I have no spots I can observe from that would allow me to shoot and move from inside the park. There are a couple of buildings outside I have as options, but nothing inside. That means a longer range shot which complicates things more. That's why I've spent this whole week so far in the shop."

Mark gestured to the fiberglass parts dangling from metal hooks in the middle of the room.

"Is that it? Your stock?" John moved closer to inspect his friends' handiwork.

"That's the first generation model. I may decide to change some things around on it later, but until I assemble everything I won't know."

"Well, it looks pretty sweet right now. I'd

love to see it when you get done."

"Oh, I'm sure you will," Mark smiled, "So, why aren't you at work, young man?"

"I took a day off to spend with Miranda today. I had to finish a few things up around the house and then decided to drop by here for a bit before picking her up. She said she had some things to do this morning as well, so I had time to kill."

"A day off? You? What ever has come over you, John?" Mark canted his head slightly and narrowed his eyes, "Why, are you in *love*?"

John grinned broadly, "Shut up. I just thought I'd burn some vacation time. I can't carry it all over to next year, you know. I have to use at least some of it up. I just thought it would be nice to do something with her instead of slouching around the house eating Apple Jacks and watching reruns this time."

"Yeah, sure. Whatever. Just be sure to invite me and the family to the wedding, Okay? Angie would be very upset if she didn't get to see you finally tie the knot." Mark chuckled.

"No, we're nowhere near that point yet. You have plenty of time to wait before you'll get that in the mail."

"So, you've at least been thinking about it, then. Interesting."

"Yeah, alright. Point made. Leave me alone," John smiled again, "Besides, I actually have other reasons to be here than to be badgered about my personal life."

"Fine. But this conversation isn't over, you know. When I tell Angie you took a day off, well, she's going to have something to say about that."

John just smiled, almost beaming from either embarrassment or happiness; perhaps a little of both. Mark really couldn't be sure.

"So what's the 'real reason' you stopped by," Mark gestured with air quotes as he pulled a seat up to the workbench.

"You may have an opportunity with the theater job."

Mark's expression became instantly more somber, "How so?"

"Scuttlebutt on the street is that a meeting

is imminent between our guy and the cartel. We don't know when or where yet, but we have some reasonable sources that say something is in the works. I'll keep you posted, but you might want to be prepared. It could be a short notice situation."

Mark scratched at his chin subconsciously.

"It wouldn't be the first time."

Chapter 11

John swung by and picked Miranda up at her apartment and they headed out to a late lunch at a little bistro near her place. The food was light but filling and they were soon engrossed in conversations about anything and everything that came up.

"I am so glad you took today off. This is going to be a lot of fun, I can tell," Miranda beamed in John's presence.

"I hope so," John replied, "I know I could use a break and spending the day with you is the icing on the cake.

"Mark has already been picking at me about it today."

"Oh, is he working at the department today?"

"No, he's at home working on a personal project. I had to stop by there for some work related stuff, though."

Miranda gazed at John, now curious as to what would take him so far out of the way for work.

"You two sure do work a lot. Doesn't it get tiresome?"

John shot her a smile, "This week has been terrible," he said, "My case load has almost doubled in recent weeks and several cases will be going to trial pretty soon. I'm down to the wire on trying to get some of them prepared for the judge.

"Meanwhile my phone won't stop ringing from people on *my* case about every one of *theirs*.

"Add to all that a new problem we've had pop up, plus the apparent vigilante that is still on the loose. I really needed a day off. I'm just glad I have you to spend it with."

Miranda studied John's face. She worried about his stress level and could see that just talking about work seemed to have an effect on him. She hoped it was a positive, therapeutic effect, but she couldn't tell.

"So, you haven't caught the one that shot the guy in the alley yet?"

John looked at her and rolled his eyes slightly, "No. Whoever he is, he's very thorough. We haven't found any evidence whatsoever and there are never any witnesses."

"So, what's the new problem that's come up? More of the same from this person?"

"No, it's different. I really shouldn't mention it, but I worry about you, especially after what happened at your shop. If I tell you, can you keep a lid on it? Please?"

"Sure," she replied, now more curious than ever.

John proceeded to tell Miranda about the situation around Carson Park with as little attention to detail as he could. He told her why they had tried to keep it quiet and how the patrols in the area were on the lookout for the man in the sketches, but he had proven to be quite elusive so far.

"Wow," was all she said.

"Promise me you'll steer clear of that part of town?"

"Oh, yeah," Miranda said with a shy smile,

"You'd have to be an idiot to go there with someone like that on the loose."

"I just hope we can get a break and catch him soon. I hate working cases like this," John shook his head and glanced across the street, not really looking for or at anything in particular.

Miranda took his hand across the tiny table and squeezed it tightly. "Don't worry about it. Something will happen. It always does. You'll get him."

"I hope so. Say, let's get out of here. I want to do things and go places with you today, not sit here and talk about work."

Miranda smiled broadly and rose from her seat, "Well, let's get started, shall we?"

Mark tightened the screws on the scope mount and carried the prototype stock and rifle assembly to his makeshift range out back of the shop. He ran through the process of attaching and detaching the barrel section a few times to get a feel for it, then grabbed a magazine and slipped it into the magazine well of the receiver. The ten round box snapped in perfectly and a sly smile crept across Himes' face.

He laid the rifle across the bench with the bolt open and proceeded to hang a bullseye target at 25 yards to zero the rifle and another at the 100 yard mark for fine tuning. Mark had decided to mount the optic directly to the barrel since the receiver would be too close to his shoulder in this configuration. Theoretically, it should be a better alignment since the scope would be in contact with the barrel instead of behind it, but he was concerned about the special mount he had built to fit the barrel. It would either work or it wouldn't and it was time for the truth to come out. Good or bad.

He extended the bipod legs from the underside of the barrel section and snuggled up to the rifle, resting his cheek on the integral brass deflector / cheek rest he had built into the stock. It fit well enough, but needed something. He'd figure that out later. First he had to make sure everything worked.

Mark ran the bolt forward on the Model 10

and locked it in. The rifle was 'hot,' the winds were calm, and he was nervous. Tenderly, Mark gripped the stock and placed his finger on the extended trigger mechanism and began to press.

With the design he had used, he could almost feel the creep as if he were using the actual trigger. It was a little spongy, but better than he expected. He took up the slack and with a little more pressure, the rifle cracked, sending a 150 grain full metal jacket downrange.

Mark ran the bolt to the rear again, ejecting the spent casing and peered through the scope. The point of impact was high and right. He adjusted the crosshairs of the Leupold scope to the left and chambered another round. With a second squeeze the rifle bucked and spat another projectile out. Once again he adjusted for windage and sent another round speeding toward the target. This time he was on horizontally. Now it was time to dial in the vertical.

He loaded a total of five rounds into the magazine and settled in behind the scope once more. Pressing the trigger Mark was beginning to feel the comfort of knowing what he had built was working. It hadn't failed to feed, fire, or eject anything yet. The barrel hadn't blown off and the stock was still in one piece.

After three more shots he had the scope zeroed and decided it was time to put the rifle through its paces. He began by threading on the suppressor and loading a full magazine of the ammo he intended to use on the job. This should require a minute adjustment from his present zero setting, but hopefully not much.

The first round of 168 grain match grade hollow point ammunition left the barrel a little slower than the 150 grain boat tailed full metal jackets, but that was to be expected. The difference in velocity and point of impact would be made up for in lethality.

The round impacted slightly low at 100 yards. Not wanting to jump to conclusions, he chambered a second, then a third round. Each impacted low center on the target, but all three holes touched. He quickly made an adjustment to the crosshairs and brought the zero point up. Three more rounds verified that the rifle was on for his preferred ammunition.

The addition of the suppressor helped to increase the velocity by about 20 percent over what it normally would have been and it decreased the sound by around 30 decibels, making the .308 sound like a .22 long rifle. Not bad, all things considered.

With the rifle impacting consecutively 2" high at 100 yards, Mark decided he could safely tuck the rifle away in the case. At that range he could calculate the ballistics for whatever distance he needed in the field.

John and Miranda strolled casually through the museum holding hands and commenting on the various artworks and historical pieces in the collections. John felt a little out of place, he had never been much one for art, but she had asked to come here, so he was happy to oblige.

After the museum they headed to the movie theater and caught what both agreed was the best superhero film to hit the box office in years. Finally the nerd in both of them was able to come out with a vengeance. Miranda couldn't help but laugh at John as he tried to play off his excitement during some of the fight sequences. He really didn't care. He was with the girl of his dreams and she was as goofy as he was at that moment. All was right with the world.

To wrap their evening up, John had pulled some strings and gotten tickets to a local comedy club. The guest comic was an up and coming star and his performance clearly showed why. At one point John saw tears streaming down Miranda's cheeks from laughter.

On the way back to her apartment, Miranda held John's hand and scooted as close to him as the console in his Jeep Wrangler would allow. She turned on the radio just as the chorus to "Best Day of My Life" by the American Authors came on. She looked at John and smiled. A more appropriate anthem to their day couldn't have been asked for.

Soon they were back in her apartment, relaxing on the couch and carrying on the way couples do when the relationship is new and fresh. John looked at his watch, "Oh, man, I need to be going. I didn't realize how late it had gotten."

"Time flies when you're having fun," Miranda said smiling; her head firmly pressed against his shoulder, "Where do you have to be tomorrow?"

"Back at work, where else?"

"Oh, just take another day off. Tell them you're sick or something."

"Uh, yeah, and do what all day? You'll be at the shop."

"I can work on contracts from here. I can also work on book sales from here, and I'm sure the one or two folks who would stop by can come some other time. Helen will just have to wait." The sarcasm in her tone was crystal clear as she giggled.

John considered it for a moment, a long moment. He had the time available. Maybe he should take another day. Dahlgren wouldn't be very happy about it, but even he'd have to admit John had earned a break.

"So," Miranda started, "What are you

thinking? Another fun-filled day with me or a boring day full of paperwork and vigilantes? I know it's a tough call." There was the giggle again. She knew she had him over a barrel and was playing it to the hilt.

"I don't know," John muttered, "Today was fun, but I really do need to get back on some of these cases."

"Party pooper," she laughed, pouting ceremoniously, but with a tiny smile at the corner of her mouth.

"Oh, I'd love to stay here and spend time with you. Believe me, you're a lot more desirable company than what I see each day at work. But, I do have a lot on the plate there and I have deadlines coming up quickly.

"I tell you what; let me get some of these cases off my desk and take care of the rapist and the vigilante and you and I will take a proper vacation together. Maybe even go and see your parents. How does that sound?"

Miranda sat straight up, surprised at the sudden decision.

"Are you sure? I mean, every time I've mentioned it before, you've never seemed interested. Why the sudden change?" Her eyes narrowed as John cracked a smile.

"I don't know. After talking to Mark today, I just got to thinking about things and, well, he has a way of getting in my head, subtly. Then spending all day with you, it just seems…right."

"Mmm hmm," came the response, "And what about your cases? Aren't they going to take a while to settle? I mean court cases can drag out for weeks."

"Nah, most of my cases are pretty cut and dry. It's just a matter of making sure the paperwork is done properly. Forget to dot an 'I' or cross a 'T' and it can be tossed out on a technicality.

"As for the vigilante and the rapist, well, I have a feeling they won't be an issue for much longer either."

Miranda sat there for a minute. She had really fallen for John and, it seemed, he had for her as well. He genuinely loved the work he did. It showed on his face as he talked about it, even when it was a bad day. He was a true protector and she knew that his protection now included her as well.

"John?"

"Yeah?"

"Can I tell you something?"

John shifted in his seat to look her in the face, "Sure, babe. What is it?"

"Well, I didn't say anything before because I just didn't want to get involved in all the mess..."

"What is it?" John could see she was getting a bit uncomfortable. She sat up facing him, her eyes cast down to the cushions of the couch. The pose reminded him of a child who had done something wrong and was waiting on a verbal reprimand.

"I, um, I was in the alley that night. He grabbed me while I was finishing my run."

John sat stunned by the revelation as Miranda continued her confession.

"I was about to go inside and get my things and go home. When I got to the alley, he just appeared and grabbed me. I didn't know what to do at first."

"Did you shoot him?"

"I never saw who shot him. He dragged me into the alley and shoved me down by the dumpster. When I looked up, the street light was behind him, so I couldn't see his face. All I knew was he was bigger and stronger than me. I managed to kick him while he fumbled with his belt and I ran.

"As I was getting into my car I thought I heard a popping sound, but I was too scared to go back. I didn't want to be anywhere near him or that alley until I knew it was safe."

John sat, speechless at first. Then the policeman part of his personality kicked in.

"You didn't see who shot him?"

"No."

"Did you hear anyone in the alley? See any shadows or notice anything out of place?"

"No. I was focused on him. My only thought was to get away and run for the car."

"Why didn't you tell anyone when we

asked before?"

John could tell that the question made her terribly uncomfortable, but it was valid and he needed an answer.

Miranda composed herself and began to recount a devastating experience.

"Five years ago, when I was working in IT, I had a job I loved. My team was great, my job was awesome. I loved everything about what I did every day. I got paid well to do it, too.

"My manager was like, the greatest guy you'd ever work for. He was always there when things got stressful. We worked on several projects that demanded long hours and a lot of sleepless nights. Well, over a period of time, our working relationship changed."

"How so?"

"Like I said, we worked closely on a number of big projects. He decided that since we worked well together, we could 'work well together' outside of the office."

"So, he made advances toward you?"

"At first it was little comments. I just

shrugged them off because I wasn't interested and he was married with kids. I just figured it was exhaustion or stress, or just you know, playful banter.

"Then they got more frequent. Soon he was just being blatant with the comments and the random hugs became more uncomfortable."

"Did you say anything to anyone?"

"Yes. I told management, but nobody would believe that he would do something like that and jeopardize his career and family. He had too much to lose.

"Anyway, one night we had been working really late. The rest of the office workers had gone home. I was trying to finish up some things and he said he was leaving for the night as well. I told him I would shut everything down since I didn't expect to stay much longer myself.

"I left the office and was heading to my car when he attacked me in the parking lot."

A tear began to stream down her left cheek and she began to fidget with her hands, wringing them as she got more visibly upset.

"I, I called the police and had charges brought, but since he had money and connections and a reputation for being such a great guy…"

"He lawyered up and the case never went to trial."

"Oh, no, we went before the judge and I felt like a fool. Between his lawyers and the lack of evidence or witnesses, I felt like a total fool.

"I swore I'd never put myself in that situation again. Ever. So, I moved here and opened the bookstore. I became my own boss and, with the connections I had through clients and other contacts, I started my contracting business.

"The system failed me, John. The system totally failed me and I never want to be a part of it again. And then you came along. You are the protector that I wish I had then."

John sat back in the seat, considering all that she had said. After a few seconds he swung back into "boyfriend" mode. Draping an arm around her shoulders he hugged her tightly, pressing her forehead into his chest.

"It's okay, babe. I didn't know. It's okay."

After a few comforting moments, she rolled her eyes up to meet his and asked, "What about your investigation? Do you *need* me to make a statement?"

John considered it all again.

"No. You didn't see the shooter or the victim's face. I don't think there's anything you can contribute. You just calm down, okay? I'm here and I'm not going to let anything happen to you."

Chapter 12

Mark woke up early and couldn't shake the dream he had about doing the theater job. His heart was still pounding as he sat on the edge of the bed. The imagery kept playing in his mind like a looped video on a department store television.

He had entered the old school building with his rifle and taken up his position in the upper floor window again. He waited until daylight and watched as the back door of the theater swung open. His man exited and Mark pulled the trigger. He missed. Not only did he miss, but he missed in a big way. Before he could chamber a second round the rooftop nests opened up on the school and soon the entire room was alive with bullets and chipping plaster.

In his dream he managed to escape the upper floor, but as he made his way out all the lower floors were filling with members of the gang. They had him trapped. His only options were to either fight his way out or jump out of an upper level window, risking injury and capture, or worse.

He turned down one of the second floor hallways and ran headlong into the dead woman from the cafeteria. She still carried the knife from the attack and was bent on revenge. Mark fired, point blank into her torso, but nothing worked. He managed to get enough of a distance that he was able to finally dive out of a window. He woke before hitting the ground.

Mark glanced at the clock. It wasn't even daylight outside yet. Angie and the kids were still fast asleep. He quietly slipped out of bed and made his way to the kitchen. Finding nothing of interest for breakfast, he scribbled a note for his wife and returned to the bedroom where he grabbed his clothes from the night before and threw them on.

Quietly tucking his keys into his pocket, Mark headed for Pancake Country. The note told Angie if she wanted him to pick anything up for herself or the kids to let him know and that he would be back later.

After a brief ride into town, Mark arrived in the parking lot to the breakfast shop and made his way inside. He pulled up a seat at the end of the bar with a good view of the dining room and began eyeing the patrons. There, in a booth to his right, sat the corporal and his wife. The old man had a quizzical expression on his face, but his wife was deeply invested in the menu.

A few seconds later the waitress stepped up to Mark's table and asked if he was ready to order.

"Yes, ma'am. I believe I'll have the number 3 plate with bacon, and hashbrowns this morning."

"How do you want your eggs, honey?"

"Scrambled, please."

"Drink?"

"Coffee will be fine. Thank you."

"Alright. I'll get this started for you and I'll be right back with a cup of coffee."

True to her word, the lady returned moments later with a cup full of steaming hot coffee and sat it on the table in front of Mark. As he doctored the beverage with sugar and creamer his eyes wandered back to the table where the older couple sat. The man now faced Mark's approximate direction and he still retained the curious look on his face. It was as if he was trying to sort something out.

"*I wonder if he knows I'm here,*" Mark thought to himself, "*That's ridiculous. Surely he couldn't have heard me all the way over there.*"

A few minutes later and the server returned to top off his coffee and let him know that the order would soon be up. Before long a gigantic plate of eggs, hashbrowns, bacon, toast, and butter sat before him with a side dish full of assorted jellies and jams.

Mark quickly went to work on the platter. He hadn't realized how hungry he was until the food had arrived, but soon it was a mere memory. He sat back in the seat and swallowed the last of his coffee before deciding it was time to go.

"Need anything else, sweetie?" The server asked in a distinctive southern drawl.

"No, I think I'm ready for the ticket," Mark said, then glanced over at the corporal, "And, would you mind if I paid for theirs as well?"

"Mr. Carver? Do you know him?"

"We recently met and I thought it would be a nice gesture."

"Do you want me to let them know you're here? They are such a sweet couple and just geniuses when it comes to gardening."

"No, no. I don't want to disturb them. I'd rather it just be an anonymous treat."

"Alright, then. If you're sure."

She turned and headed for the register. Soon she reappeared beside the table with a pair of paper slips in her hand.

"Here you go, honey. Whenever you're ready just come up to the register and we'll check you out."

"Thank you," Mark said, "Say, can you tell me anything else about Mr. Carver?"

"Oh, he's hilarious. I think he used to be in the military and, well, he can tell some stories. I think he went blind several years after he came home from the service. Some say it's because of something he was exposed to while he was over there, but I don't know.

"Anyway, his nephew was in the military too, but he was killed. You'd have to ask him about the details on that, though. I never knew what happened. Afterwards, they stepped in and helped his niece raise her son. They were almost like the parents since she spent all her time working to pay the bills."

"What about them? Any kids of their own?"

"No. I think that's why they were so eager to help out with their nephew. He was like the kid they never had."

"Oh, OK. I don't mean to be nosy, but, like you said, he's an interesting fellow."

"No trouble at all. I need to go bus this table. If you need anything else, let me know, OK?"

Mark nodded as she turned back to her work. He sat there for a few minutes and calculated the total and tips for both tabs, then stood and stretched before heading to the cashier.

Mark decided that he would make a quick trip to the restroom before getting back on the road home, so he made his way to the far end of the establishment and went inside. As he stood at the sink, washing his hands, the door swung open and James Carver, the corporal, sauntered in with a wooden cane in one hand.

"Hello there," he said with a smile across his face, "Good to see you again."

Mark smiled as the man chuckled.

"Good to see you too. I notice that you got your wife to skip cooking breakfast again this morning."

"Number one job of the day, son. How do you think I got to live this long?"

Mark laughed at the thought of the woman's cooking being worse than a combat tour in Vietnam.

Carver stepped over to the adjacent sink and turned the water on.

"Okay," Mark began, "How did you know I was here? I'm not wearing wet shoes today."

Carver smiled, "I caught a whiff of you

when you walked by. You smelled like someone I met in my back yard recently."

He reached for the paper towel dispenser as Mark cranked a fresh sheet out for him.

"Thank you, son. What brings you out here on such a fine morning?"

"Having trouble sleeping. Thought I might as well get something to eat and for some reason this just seemed like the place to go."

Carver grinned, "They do have good food here. How's 'work' going for you?"

Himes stammered for a minute, glancing at the stalls to see if anyone else was within earshot.

"It's…going. Kind of hit a bit of a wall moving forward right now, but something will work out, I'm sure."

"Things may work out better than you think. And sooner, too," the old man continued.

Mark's expression became very serious.

"How do you mean?"

Carver leaned a little forward, the cane under his palms.

"I overheard a couple of those folks two

mornings ago as they strolled through my yard talking about a meeting. Seems they have some important people coming in for a visit pretty soon; maybe within the next six weeks or so. Someone's coming from Mexico or something. All I know is they seemed pretty concerned about it."

Mark processed the information quickly and began reaching for his wallet. Rummaging around in the folds of it he found what he was looking for.

"If you hear anything else, can you call this man? He's a friend of mine. I'd appreciate it."

Himes handed the man a business card of John's. Carver held it up just a couple of inches from his eyes.

"A cop? I don't know about that. I don't need any cops hanging around my house. You've seen where I live, right?"

"He's a cop, yes, but he and I have known each other for years. He's not going to come and visit and won't send anyone else to either. He's the best way to get information to me. Well, unless you'd rather I camp out in your begonias."

"Don't be messin' with my flowers, now," Carver smiled as he handed John's card back, "I got the number. If I hear anything, I'll call."

"You don't need the card?"

"I said I got the number, didn't I? Now, just leave an old man alone about it. My wife's going to think I got stuck or something if I don't get back out there."

Mark laughed and reached for the door.

"One more thing, son," The corporal commented, "I have a nephew. He fell in with those idiots down there. I know it's a lot to ask, but, well, if it all goes sideways…"

"I'll try to keep him out of my sights. I'll need to know what he looks like, though."

"His name is Adam Robinson. They call him A-Rob. Stupid name, if you ask me. You can probably get a better picture of him from your friend. He's done some stupid stuff before."

"I'll see what I can find," Mark said, "You know, I can't promise anything if it gets crazy out there."

"I just don't want him hurt. I also know

that everything happens for a reason. Sometimes that reason is you are stupid and make bad decisions. He made a bad decision hooking up with those folks. If you can get him away from them, I'd appreciate it. If not, I understand."

"I'll try my best, sir."

"What did I tell you about callin' me 'sir'?"

Mark just smiled and opened the door.

On the way home Himes got called to the precinct to replace some light bulbs and work on an office door that had taken a beating during a booking. A rather belligerent drunk had made his mind up that he didn't want to stay the night in the drunk tank. When he eyed the comfortable chair and large computer monitor in the office, he concluded that it must be a hotel room and deftly made his way toward it, taking two officers with him. After a few minutes of some considerable pounding against, and almost through, the door, he was convinced to go to the tank and sober up.

Mark arrived at the police station and quickly set himself to work replacing the light bulbs first. Most were out in the main office area, above the cubicles used by the detectives and others. It was early enough that many of them hadn't come in yet, but the place was still somewhat lively.

The last bulbs he changed were actually in the Chief's office. Mark knocked on the door, a little surprised to see the aged law man in at such an early hour.

"Come in, Mark. Good to see you. Here to change my bulbs?"

"Yes, sir. I'd hate for you not to be able to see what you're doing."

"Heh," the man chuckled, "Some days I wish I didn't have to see any of it. Here, let me move this chair out of your way."

"I've got it, sir. No trouble at all."

Mark slid the chair off to the side and noticed the map full of pins hanging on the wall nearby. He stared for just a moment when Dahlgren's voice grumbled again.

"Crimes. Each one of those pins is a different crime committed in our city just this year.

Blue ones are domestic calls, yellow ones are property thefts, greens are vehicular theft, white ones are for assaults, and red ones are homicides."

"Whoa," Mark said marveling at the sheer number of pins on the map, "That's a lot of pins."

"Hmm," Dahlgren grunted, "And the year isn't over yet. If this economy doesn't turn around and people find work we'll have thieves stealing from thieves. Hell, we've already got that now, but it will be worse."

Mark turned around and noticed that beside his desk, mounted to the wall, was a small television. The volume was down, but not so much that the news broadcast couldn't be heard.

Behind the anchor's left shoulder was a piece of financial clipart. Apparently that was the topic of the morning on the news set as well.

"...In related news, President Hawthorne announced yesterday that he is forming a new Congressional Committee to evaluate additional measures to stimulate the economy. The President has been in negotiations with the chairman of the Federal Reserve in recent weeks in an attempt to keep interest rates low and avoid any further quantitative easing efforts. Sources in the White House have suggested that one of the options on the table could be additional fuel tax hikes and possibly new taxes on property and large businesses…."

"You know, I had high hopes for that idiot when he ran," Dahlgren said, "I voted for the man because he wasn't a career politician. He was a successful businessman with an impressive track record of creating jobs and developing industries. I thought he'd be the shot in the arm this country needed to get back on its feet. Now I'm afraid it was a shot in the dark and he hasn't got a clue what he's doing."

"Don't feel bad, sir. I know you're not the only one who has gotten tired of the same old routine. I didn't vote *for* him so much as I voted *against* the other guy. The lesser of two evils, you might say."

Dahlgren nodded his head in agreement as Mark moved his ladder into position to change the bulbs.

A short time later he put the ladder away

and began evaluating the damage to the door. The hinge screws had become loose, so he would simply replace them with some longer ones to bite a little better into the jamb. A simple fix, but he'd have to get a drill and driver bit plus the screws he needed in order to make it work.

The drill and bit were in the supply room, but he couldn't find any screws suitable for the task so he decided to make a quick trip to the nearest hardware store.

As he headed for the truck he saw John coming in. He looked terrible, as if he hadn't slept all night.

"Hey, man. You OK?" Mark asked his old friend.

"I'm fine. It was just a late night. I didn't get much sleep."

Mark shot him a glance with a dirty smile.

"No. We stayed up pretty late talking. Pervert."

Mark laughed, finally urging a small smile from John.

"You remember the question about baggage? Well, I found it last night."

"Uh oh," Mark said, "Was it that bad?"

John yawned like a lion on an Animal Planet documentary.

"No, not really. Something that happened a few years ago. It just kind of caught me off guard, you know?"

Mark just nodded his head with a curious expression.

"Hey, I need to run and get some screws for that door over there. I'll catch up to you when I'm done, okay? That'll give you a little time to wake up."

"Yeah, waking up would be good," John said through another gigantic yawn, "I need my coffee." He stumbled toward the break room and the coffee maker.

Before long, Mark returned with the screws he needed and within minutes the door was properly functioning again. He put his tools away and decided it was time to seek out John for an update on the dating situation.

He found Thompson sitting at his desk a

couple of doors down from Dahlgren's office with a large cup of coffee within reach.

"You awake yet?"

"Yeah, come on in. Grab a chair."

Mark stepped into the room and pulled a chair up across the desk from John.

"Want some coffee or anything?"

Mark considered it, but decided that he was still pretty full from breakfast.

"Nah, I got the number 3 plate at Pancake Country before I came here. I'm still stuffed. Thanks for the offer, though."

"Wow," John began, "That's a lot of food. What brings you into town that early in the morning?"

"Couldn't sleep," Mark cut his eyes over to the doorway, wondering if he should say any more about his conversation with Carver.

John caught the cursory glance and stood to close the door. As he returned to his seat he asked, "So, just having trouble sleeping, huh?"

"Nightmares, all about that theater. It's bugging me like no other job has. I gotta be honest, John, I haven't figured a good way to do this one yet. It's kind of pissing me off."

John sat back in his chair a moment.

"Remember, we may have an opportunity if our information is correct. If this meeting happens, we could catch him and possibly another big fish in the same barrel."

"Yeah, about that," Mark said, "I may have developed a contact in the neighborhood myself. He basically told me the same thing. There's a meeting with someone from Mexico or somewhere that's coming soon. Within the next six weeks."

"Do you trust the source?"

"I think so. He's an older man, blind; a corporal from the Vietnam War. He's quite a character."

"Blind, huh? So you don't think he can identify you?"

Mark recounted his initial encounter with Carver and then told of the meeting this morning and how he had given Carver John's card as a contact.

"There's one other thing," Mark continued, "I need a good picture of his nephew. Carver told me you could help with that."

Soon John had the young man's image on the screen and printed Mark a copy.

"That should help a lot," he said, "I don't know if I can live up to Carver's expectations, but I have to at least try.

"So, what is all this about staying up late on a school night, young man?"

John smiled and told Mark about the events of the day before, including Miranda's past that kept him up all night. He explained that she was the victim in the alleyway where the man was killed outside her shop, but couldn't identify either the victim or the shooter, so he was going to let her statement go.

Mark thought about it for a minute.

"You know," he said, "That morning I saw the blonde being assaulted by those two thugs, it was very similar."

"How so?"

"Well, the girl was cornered in an alley.

They had her, no doubt. I heard shots and the girl came running out. I watched for a while to try and see if anyone else came out, but I never saw any other movement. Maybe the shooter was still in the alley, cleaning up the scene and I just didn't wait long enough." Mark sat back in the chair, a little frustrated with himself for his lack of patience.

"Was the girl carrying a weapon? Could she have been the shooter?"

"If she was the shooter, I'd like to know where she put the gun," Mark smiled, "The outfit she was wearing didn't leave much to the imagination, so I don't know where she could have put any kind of weapon.

"No, I'd say there had to be someone else in that alley."

John sat silently for a moment.

"Isn't it funny, though," he began, "that the vigilante would just happen to be in the right place at the right time?"

"Could be you have the city's first real superhero out there." Mark smiled.

Further Reduction

"Yeah, well, he's on your list too."

Chapter 13

On his third trip into the neighborhood around the theater, Mark decided to go to the south side and observe from a rooftop position. Again, he parked in the garage and carefully made his way in before sunrise.

The building of choice was a couple of blocks away from the front of the theater, closer than he had been before, but far enough away that he figured he could be fairly safe from prying eyes.

The three story building was once a department store of sorts and probably provided many of the locals a source for all manner of dry goods. A sturdy, almost stately building, its windows were long gone and graffiti now covered a good portion of what was once an ad for Coca Cola painted directly onto the bricks.

As Himes approached the building he became aware of an increase in the number of people on the streets. Fortunately, they acted as if the patrols had become mundane time killers, so their observations were sloppy, at best. Still, you didn't have to look as hard if there were more people looking, so he kept to the shadows and used the monocular often.

From across the street he saw activity in the main floor of his building. That wasn't good. Even a vagrant could give him away. Time to fall back to his second choice. It was a two story number about a block farther south, but he had no other option. He immediately made for the building.

Again he sat across the street for a few minutes before approaching to be sure there wasn't any movement inside. He entered the building through a side door that was off its hinges and scouted for a stairway. He soon found it toward the rear of the building and it didn't look very promising.

Carefully picking his way up the creaky staircase he made it to the second floor and scanned for occupants and roof access. A couple of mice scurried into their respective holes, but no other creatures inhabited the building at the moment. Mark found the ladder in a small room against the back wall and proceeded to climb up.

He gingerly stepped across the roof, which sagged in several places from years of neglect and weather damage. From up there he could clearly see the rooftop emplacements on the theater and the street out front. He kept low to the roof, hiding behind the small wall around the perimeter as much as possible. Himes noted everything he saw again, like the previous two trips in. Many of his observations were the same, but there were more people and more activity tonight than before.

Having to change his plans for a secondary location had taken time out of his opportunity to observe, so he would have to be on the move earlier than planned. He definitely didn't want to be caught this close with his bag of tricks.

The time finally came for him to exfiltrate and go home. He began tucking his notepad and pencil away and something caught his attention on the theater roof. Himes quickly swung the spotting scope around and focused on it

He could see, through the gloom, a large box, the lid opened toward his position. Around it stood three people, men, he assumed, but he didn't dare want to put money on it after the masculine woman he had encountered before.

Soon they produced something from the container that Mark never expected.

"Oh, you've *got* to be kidding me," Mark sighed to himself.

The drone was a big quadcopter design complete with an HD camera dangling on a gimbal beneath. Soon the limbs of the aircraft came alive with glowing red and green LED light as one of the individuals stepped off to the side to give clearance for liftoff.

Mark grabbed his gear and shuffled quickly toward the ladder. All he needed was to be caught on camera. He didn't know if the thing had night vision capability or not, but he wasn't going to take the time to find out.

In his haste he didn't have time to check the roof for stability and soon his left foot found a soft spot, punching clear through the old roofing material and sending chunks of water damaged wood down into the upper floor making a raucous crash.

Himes yanked the foot free and raced to the ladder. Within seconds he was back inside and making his way down the shoddy staircase.

With a quick glance out a nearby window he could see the glowing lights on the drone as it came closer to the building. He ducked behind a small wall and held his breath. Maybe they hadn't seen him. Maybe they hadn't heard. Maybe they were just playing around and trying to learn how they could use the thing.

It swung over the building next to his and then began a return to the theater, veering out over the street in front as it did. Mark took the chance and moved.

Soon he was on the ground and sprinting across the street. His heart was racing as the drone proceeded to the north side of the theater. A small sigh of relief came out as Himes realized he had not been spotted by the new sentry. He began his move out of the area and back to the truck.

Stepping into a small alleyway, Himes decided to be safe he would put on his face mask and thread the suppressor onto the 1911. He didn't want to run the risk of being unprepared like he had been in the cafeteria.

He moved as quickly and quietly as his pace would allow toward the parking garage, trying to keep a wide berth around the streets closest to the theater. Sweeping the areas in front of him with the monocular was effective, but his adrenaline was pumping and he was careless enough to be spotted.

"Hey!" Mark knew the voice wasn't Carver. He dodged behind a large Boxwood shrub and brought the .45 out.

"I know he's over here somewhere," a voice mumbled.

"Who was it? Could you see him?"

"Nah, Couldn't see his face, but he hid, and that means he ain't one of us."

The voices got slowly closer to Mark's position. He debated trying to sweep around the house and cross the road into the shadows on the opposite side, but didn't think he'd have time.

"Think we ought to call it in?"

"I want to know who it is first. Could be nuthin'," the first voice said.

"Could be something," the second voice replied.

"Just shut up, man. Shut up and be quiet."

The two men were almost on him. Mark stepped back around the corner of the house and eased toward the opposite side. A few more steps and he'd make a run for it.

Quietly he slipped to the front yard and scanned the street with the monocular. No signs of movement anywhere. He could hear the two men around the back of the house and decided it was time to make a break for it.

Mark broke the cover of the house and shrubbery and sprinted across the pavement. His feet hit heavily enough on the ground that the men heard him on the move and raced around the house in pursuit.

He turned down a narrow back street and zigzagged around trash cans and boxes in a mad dash for a secure outlet. Suddenly, up ahead, a figure stepped out in front of him and raised a weapon. Himes swung the 1911 up and squeezed the trigger without missing a step. The suppressed hollow point impacted the man in the throat, severing the spinal column on the left side and tearing out tissue and veins as it deflected off the bone. Without a further sound the man was down and immobile, his rifle still in his grip.

Himes stopped just past the man and evaluated his position quickly. As he studied his options, he heard the second man approach from his right. Apparently the man hadn't heard the shot and didn't know his partner was down or he would have been on the radio and calling in assistance

Mark squatted silently in the shadow of a dumpster as the man stepped out in front of him. Himes quickly smacked the man in the back of the head with the pistol, knocking him out cold. In the dimness of the street lights he rolled the man over and looked at his face.

"My luck just gets better all the time," he

mumbled to himself as he stared at the face of Adam Robinson.

Robinson woke a few minutes later in a groggy state with a splitting headache to find he was securely tied to a straight back chair inside the old church building. Directly in front of him, sitting on a pew, was a strange man with a facemask covering his visage. From the eyes he could tell the man was Caucasian, but any other features were obscured. The man sat in the shadows, so he couldn't even be sure of eye or hair color.

"How's your head?" the man asked.

"What the hell did you hit me with, a tank?"

The dark figure chuckled lightly.

"Look, I don't have a whole lot of time, so I'm going to get right to the point. You have a choice to make. Right now. Get out of this gang and do something positive with your life, or I'm going to kill you like I did your partner in the alley."

"What? You killed Billy? You son of a…"

"NOW!" the man shouted, "I need an answer form you, right now. You have people out there that are worried about you; that care about you. That's the only reason you are alive right now and I need an answer."

Robinson was thoroughly confused.

"Who are you? Why are you doin' this?"

"I'm nobody you want to be on the bad side of and you're getting there quickly."

"But, who are you? What are you talkin' about?"

The man stood, his body still concealed by the shadows.

"Alright, screw this. I'm out of time."

Robinson heard the distinctive sound of a pistol slide cycle and saw the man raise the suppressed 1911, pointing it directly at his face.

"Whoa, whoa, wait a minute, man! Wait a minute!"

"Why?" The man asked as if killing him was no different than turning off a light.

"Look man, you don't just 'leave' alright? I can't just go and turn in a notice like I'm quitting a job or something. That ain't how it works."

"Well, you need to figure something out. I can shoot you here and leave you in this building to rot or I can turn you loose to do the right thing. The choice is yours."

Robinson thought about it hard for a moment. He was infuriated at the man for killing his friend. He wanted to break out of the chair and use the ropes to strangle the shadowy figure, but at the same time he knew he was right. The years of living with his aunt and uncle hadn't faded completely. He remembered how his uncle taught him about honor and duty. He remembered how his aunt had always encouraged him to get out of the neighborhood and do something good for himself. She always pushed him to do better; to *be* better.

"You talked to my family, didn't you?"

"They're worried about you. They want you to come home. The choice is yours."

Robinson stared at the man, then dropped his eyes to the floor in silence. Inside he was an emotional roller coaster of anger and frustration coupled with the fear of disappointment his family must be feeling over his choices. What would his mother say if she could be here right now? Thankfully she had passed away and couldn't see the man he had become.

"Alright. Fine. I'll go and talk to my uncle. Maybe he can help me figure out what to do."

"Smart kid," the shadowy man said in a low voice, "Now, I need to be going."

"You gonna cut me loose?"

The man turned and picked up Robinson's rifle and magazines.

"You know, I'd really love to do that. I really would. But I just don't trust you not to try something stupid. I'm funny that way."

"What? You just gonna leave me here? Tied to a chair?"

The man reached behind a pew and pulled something out. He walked toward Robinson and tossed a dusty Bible in his lap.

"Here's a little something to keep you company until your friends show up. Or you figure out how to loosen the zip ties. Happy reading."

With that the man slipped out the back

door leaving Robinson alone in the church, bathed in the glow of the street light as it shined through one of the only remaining stained glass windows.

Chapter 14

It was a beautiful Saturday to be outside. The balmy 74 degree temperature played host to a gentle southwestern breeze and there was hardly a cloud in the sky.

Mark and Andy busied themselves with pasting targets while Angie and Ashley stayed under the shelter at the range.

"Tape," Mark said to the youth.

"OK," was the reply as Andy tore a small roughly one inch section off the roll.

"Not bad, dude, not bad. We need to work on that eye dominance, though."

"Eye what?"

"Dominance. It means one eye is stronger and more likely to be used than the other for sighting your rifle. Or, in your case, your BB gun."

"What difference does it make?"

"Well, when you shoot, you pull the trigger with your right hand, but you try to look down the sights with your left eye. That puts your head in an awkward position and can make your accuracy suffer."

"So I need to shoot with my left hand?"

"It would be easier to train you to use your right eye. Besides, most guns are designed around right handed shooters."

"But, what if someone is left handed? Can they not own a gun?"

Mark smiled at his son and the mature line of questions he posed for an eight year old.

"No, they make left handed guns, they just don't make as many."

"Well, that's kind of dumb."

"Not really," Mark laughed, "There just aren't as many left handed shooters as right handed shooters, so they don't sell as many left handed guns. Manufacturers don't want to have a lot of guns sitting around that they can't sell. You see?"

"But what if I want to buy a certain kind of gun and they only make it for right handed people?"

"I'm sure you could probably find a left handed model. It just might take a little looking."

"What about one like Sissy's?" He referred to the .22 caliber AR-15 that his older sister had been practicing with.

"Ah," Mark began with his finger pointed in the air, "That type of gun can be what's called 'ambidextrous.'"

"Ambi-what?"

"Ambidextrous. It means you can shoot it either left or right handed. That's what a lot of guns are now."

"So," Andy studied the concept as the question formulated, "if you can shoot it either left or right handed, does that mean you can shoot it either left or right eyed too?"

"It would still be better to use the right eye. You know, I know a few people that are left handed and have trained themselves to shoot right handed. One or two are particularly good.

"Then I know several people who shoot, or shot, like you; left eye dominant."

"Are they any good?"

"Oh yeah. Some of those guys are *very* good. But, they trained themselves to shoot with their non-dominant eye."

Andy thought about it for a bit. It sounded like learning. He didn't care much for learning, but he did like to target practice with his BB gun. Maybe learning something to help him shoot it better wouldn't be too bad.

"How do you train your eyes? I mean, change the dominance?"

"It's pretty simple. You can either close your left eye when you shoot until you get comfortable sighting with your right eye all the time, or you can cover the lens on your safety glasses so you can't see through it."

"I can close my eye really easy, see?"

Mark chuckled at Andy's gesture.

"Well, I think it might be better in the long run to cover the lens. That way you don't develop the habit of closing your eye. Sometimes keeping both eyes open is really important."

A curious expression crossed Andy's face, "Why? We're just on the range."

"Yes," Mark replied, "but even on the range you need to be able to see what's happening around you. If someone walked up as you were about to shoot to tell you something important you might not see them. Things like that."

Andy nodded his head as the pair reached the bench again.

"How did my little marksman do?" Angie asked.

"Good," Andy said with a smile, "but I gotta work on my eye dominance. That's when you look at the sights crooked."

"Angie," Mark said as he smiled at Andy's summary, "Grab your gear and let's go. You're up."

"But I'm so comfortable here in the shade," she pouted her lower lip out as she sat her soft drink down in the cup holder of the chair.

"You can get back in the shade in a minute. We need to work on your grip and stance. Fundamentals, young lady. Fundamentals."

"Yeah, mom," Ashley chimed in, "I could outshoot you. You need practice."

Angie turned to face the smiling lass with her jaw open and a look of shock on her face.

"Is that a *challenge?*"

Both girls smiled

"Yep."

"Me too, me too," Andy piped up.

"Looks like things are about to get interesting. I'll tell you what," Mark said, "Let me work with mommy for a minute and then you can start the competition. I'll judge. Losers have to wash the dishes tonight."

Suddenly a change of expression crossed both kids' faces as they realized what they had started. Ashley broke the awkward silence.

"Deal."

Andy shot her a look that showed his concern for her sanity.

"Count me out," he said. He had already figured that his sister was counting on him being one of the two losers and all she would then have to do would be shoot better than their mother. He wasn't sure if she could, but he wasn't willing to take the chance. In his eyes it was a losing situation for him no matter what.

"What does the winner get?" Ashley queried.

Mark studied the question momentarily but Angie spoke up before he could decide on a prize.

"Bragging rights," She smiled. The look on Ashley's face dimmed.

"And the choice of what we do tonight for Family Night."

The smile returned to the girl's face. Mark instantly knew it was going to be something he either didn't want to do, or something he really didn't want to spend the money on. Maybe Angie would win.

As they negotiated the terms of the competition, John pulled up in his Jeep and began to unload his range bag. To everyone's surprise Miranda hopped out of the passenger side seat with a wave.

"Hi, guys," she said with a grin, "Fancy meeting you here."

After exchanging salutations the two groups united under the shade of the shelter to swap pleasantries.

"What brings you two out today?" Angie asked.

"John said he wanted me to work on my concealed carry permit. He's worried about my safety after what happed outside my shop."

"You ever shoot any more, Miranda?" Mark asked, knowing she used to heft a rifle when she was home on the ranch.

"It's been a while. When I was younger I would shoot rifles a lot on the family farm, but that's been a few years."

"Well, today we're going to work on your pistol skills," John interjected as he produced a couple of plastic boxes from inside the bag, "It's kind of hard to conceal a rifle." He gave Mark a cursory glance and smile.

Mark didn't say a word. He only smiled back and glanced at the handgun selection John had provided.

"Don't let us interrupt," Miranda said, "We've got all day and you guys look like you're about to do some serious target practice," she gestured to the targets all along the backstop.

"Mommy and Ashley are going to fight over who does the dishes tonight," Andy said, a toothy grin across his face.

"Mark, are you not going to get in on that action," John smiled again, "or are you afraid you'll lose?"

"I'm sitting this one out. You haven't seen these two shoot and I'm not a big fan of dishpan hands."

Mark asked John if he could help him retrieve some of the steel targets from the nearby storage shed. As the duo stepped away from the rest of the group John updated Mark on a few items of interest.

"We checked into the casualties from the theater and school. Both had extensive sheets, but not much in the way of felonies until recently. Mostly drug charges, theft, some assaults, and prostitution."

"Prostitution?" Mark thought about the woman in the cafeteria and her mannish appearance, then the man in the alleyway, "Which one?"

"The woman," John laughed, "Yeah, I had to think about it too. She wasn't exactly what you'd call a typical street walker, but I guess when you need money you do what you have to do. It's a weird world, man.

"Anyway," he continued as he started pulling a dueling tree from the small room, "You will be getting a little payout for those in a couple of days. The big fish is still the one we want, but taking out an army can be expensive too. The Chief is still trying to set up a method of payment for that one. He's asked if there is any way to get the cartel man too. Any ideas?"

Himes studied the notion for a moment.

"It's hard to be in two places at once, you know. Maybe, if I can catch them both outside at the theater, but that might give my position away. Let me do some figuring. I'll come up with something.

"Do you need pepper poppers for your work with Miranda?"

"Yeah, help me drag a couple of those out if you don't mind."

They soon had the dueling tree in position for Angie and Ashley to use in their contest while Miranda's steel popper targets for her handgun training were set up to the side.

Mark and Angie took a few minutes to work on her grip and stance, getting her comfortable with the Glock 19 she carried on her hip. After a brief refresher, Angie was drilling targets regularly and rapidly. Mark glanced over at his daughter who was watching the demonstration with casual interest.

Afterwards Mark changed out the upper half on another AR-15 to a .22 Long Rifle caliber so that both girls could have an even playing field. Angie ran several rounds through it to get comfortable with the feel and operation before she announced that she was ready for the competition.

The rules were very simple. Each shooter would have two magazines full of .22 ammo. They would have 30 seconds to engage the dueling tree, after which they would move to the targets out at 50 yards and expend the remaining ammo in the magazines.

Further Reduction

Whoever had the most flipped targets on the dueling tree plus the highest score on the ringed bullseye targets would win the contest. In the event of a tie, both shooters would get a single shot on the bullseye targets to see who could hit a higher point value ring.

The competitors took seats at the bench and lined up on their dueling tree.

"Shooters ready?" Mark asked.

"Ready," they replied in unison.

He glanced around the shed to make sure everyone had their proper eye and ear safety on, then turned back to the bench. With a press of the button on the stopwatch he called, "Go!"

The next 30 seconds were a flurry of shots with the small hinged disks of the tree flipping first to the left, then to the right, then back to the left, exposing the different colored sides as rounds impacted each one. Ashley had to change the magazine in her rifle but as she did, her mother flipped the targets back over, increasing her score.

"Mom!" Ashley snapped as she charged the weapon. Her mother continued to fire with a smug grin on her face.

Now it was Angie's time to reload and Ashley smiled at her mother's inconvenience.

Ashley managed to flip almost half of the targets back over before time ran out.

"Time!" Mark called as the sights shifted to the paper targets.

The pace of fire had slowed noticeably as each carefully picked their shots and tried to hit the smaller, higher value, centers.

Ashley emptied her magazine and dropped the empty box from the magazine well, flipping the safety and sitting back in her seat as she did so.

Within a few seconds, Angie did the same.

"Time to tally it up," Mark said with a smile.

The dueling tree had four of the six targets flipped in Angie's favor, only beating Ashley by a single target.

The score on the paper was much farther apart with Ashley thoroughly defeating her mother's score. There was no need to even count it, really, since most of the center was eaten away from Ashley's target and many of Angie's had fallen low into the outer rings. Mark collected the targets and returned to the table.

"Sorry, honey," he said, "Looks like you get to do the dishes tonight."

Angie's jaw dropped as she looked at the gaping hole in her daughter's target. Ashley grinned from ear to ear before turning to her mother and sticking her tongue out.

"Told you. You need more practice," she smiled, "Now I get to decide what we do for tonight!"

John and Miranda were both amazed at Ashley's accuracy.

"Looks like you've got quite the protégé there," John said.

"You told me she was good," Angie stammered, "I didn't know you meant that good."

"You should have known something was up when I didn't want to shoot," Mark said as he gave Angie a comforting hug.

"I know!" Ashley proudly announced, "I want to go see that new Marvel movie and eat at

Bonefish Grill!"

Angie didn't say a word. Mark immediately began to estimate the cost of the evening. It would be pricey, taking the whole family for dinner and a movie, but at least they could swing it now. Things weren't as tight as when he'd first lost his job.

"Are you sure?" Mark asked, his eyes narrowed.

"Yep. We haven't been there in so long, and I love the big paper table cloths that you can draw on. That's where I want to go. Plus, I'm tired of waiting for all the good movies to come out on video. I want to see one in an actual theater for a change."

Angie and Mark shot each other a quick glance, without a word understanding each other and agreeing.

"Done," Mark said with a smile.

"And I don't have to do dishes tonight," Angie said with a grin.

Chapter 15

Jenny Carver opened the front door and a smile immediately washed over her face.

"Adam?"

"Hi, Aunt Jenny. Can I come in for a minute?"

"You know you can. Do you want something to eat or drink? Go sit down in the living room, your Uncle James is in there listening to the radio," She turned her head in the direction of the living room and called, "James! Adam's home!"

With a beaming smile across her face the elderly lady escorted the prodigal nephew into the house and nudged him to a chair in the small living room as she made her way to the kitchen.

There, sitting in a well worn recliner, cane by the armrest, sat his uncle. Despite his age, James Carver was an imposing figure, especially when he had been the father figure for years.

With as much respect as he could muster,

Adam addressed the patriarch as he took a seat in the chair and laid his bag on the floor by his feet.

"Hi, Uncle James."

The man sat stone-like, uttering only a soft grunt of acknowledgement.

Robinson knew his uncle wasn't sure what to make of his sudden appearance and, rightfully so, questioned his motives.

Adam cleared his throat, trying to formulate what he wanted to say. He wasn't quite sure where to begin.

Jenny appeared from the kitchen with three glasses of lemonade on a small tray. In the middle of the tray sat a stack of cookies, probably homemade. She strode into the room with a glowing face and sat on the couch, completing the conversational triangle.

She passed out the drinks and informed everyone, mainly James, that there were cookies to be had as well. She knew that he couldn't hold his stoic disposition long when cookies were in the room.

"You always know, don't you?" James said,

cracking a tiny smile at his wife.

"Well, it's too quiet in here. Someone had to do something."

Adam smiled at the couple. He hadn't lived here, hadn't even set foot in the house, for a few years, yet some things never seemed to change.

Jenny handed James a cookie and sat back in her seat, cutting her eyes toward the younger man.

"So, Adam, what brings you by? Is everything OK?"

James sat silently, still sizing the nephew up.

"Well, I needed to talk to you. Both of you, about something really important," Adam began, "Mostly I needed to talk to Uncle James." He cut his eyes at his uncle with a hint of hope on his face.

"Go on," the elder finally said. The tone was almost that of a regal king upon his throne.

Adam swallowed a big drink of lemonade, still trying to decide where to begin.

"I ran into your friend about a week ago,"

he said. Jenny looked a little confused, but didn't say a word.

"How'd that work out for you?" James was now very interested in why the young man sat in his living room.

"He gave me a lot to think about. A whole lot," Adam cast his eyes down to the small pack he carried with him.

"I'll bet," James commented.

"Yeah," Adam continued, "Me and Billy were out patrolling that morning. We saw him cutting across the yards, heading away from the theater. Someone had been in a building spying on us at the theater, so we were told to find out who it was. We managed to catch up to him, but he shot Billy in a back alley. I never heard a shot. I never saw Billy again, but he said he shot him."

"You weren't with Billy?"

"We split up to try and get on either side of him. We figured if we had him cornered we could find out who he was and what he was doing.

"Anyway, I got around in front of him and as I walked past a dumpster he hit me in the head.

I don't remember anything after that."

James began to smile.

"Who?" Jenny asked, a tone of protective concern in her voice, "Who hit you in the head? What's this all about, James?"

Carver simply held up his hand and calmly said, "Calm down, Jenny. Let the boy finish talking," he turned his attention back to his nephew, "He certainly has a way of making a first impression, doesn't he?"

"Yeah, yeah he does," Robinson said, subconsciously rubbing the spot on his head, "Anyway, when I woke up, I was in the old church a couple of blocks away. He had me tied to a chair. He was waiting on me to wake up. I don't know how long I was out, but he just sat there in the pews until I came to.

"I asked him who he was and what was going on. He told me that the only reason I was still alive was because he had talked to you."

"Oh, James!" Jenny declared.

Another reassuring hand from James helped to calm her exasperation, outwardly at least.

"Anyway, He told me I needed to make a choice. He said that I could either straighten up and leave the gang, or he'd kill me right then and there."

"Who was this man? We need to call the police!" Jenny was beyond agitated at the idea of anyone treating her nephew that way.

"Calm down, Jenny. Nobody's calling the police for anything. I'm sure they already know about Billy and Adam's fine. If they want the man, they'll already be looking for him," James grinned at Adam, "So, what made you want to come here?"

Adam looked a bit uncomfortable as he shifted his position and picked the bag up off the floor.

"Well," he said, "At first, when he told me that, I was just mad. I wanted to kill him. I wanted to get out of that chair and kill him, right there. Then I got to thinking about it. About what he said. About him talking to you and you being worried about me. About how you were the only reason he didn't kill me already and that the decision to stay alive was up to me."

He looked at his aunt and cast his eyes to the floor, shamefully.

"I've messed up. I made a lot of dumb decisions. I left everything you taught me growing up because I thought it was better to have money and people that treated me like friends. They aren't my friends. They never were."

"So, what did you tell him?"

Adam looked at his uncle. The old man's expression was still as stony as it was when he first entered the room.

"I told him I'd leave. That I would get out of what I was in, but I needed to figure out how. You don't just leave. It's not like that. It's not that easy."

"So, if it's not that easy, what do you expect us to do? Call your leader tell him you won't be coming back? Do you need a note?" James' sarcasm was on a roll.

Adam snorted lightly as a small smile crossed his face.

"No," he said, "I don't think that would

work either.

"I know you've been in some tight spots before. When you were in the Marines, you had to think on your feet a lot. You were in some bad places more than once, and you survived. You got out. I figure if you can live through all that, you can help me figure out how to get out of my spot."

James sat in his chair silently. Memories of Vietnam popped on and off in his mind as he considered Adam's words.

"Son," he finally began, "I was in some tough situations there, that's true. And, yes, I did make it out. But a lot of good men didn't. Dear friends of mine, close friends, died in those rice paddies and jungles. Sometimes I think I'm the exception to the rule."

Adam measured the comment with growing pangs of desperation. He knew he had to change, he just didn't know how. Any help would be better than no help.

"Let me think about it," James said finally, "I know, between the three of us, we can come up with something. But you're going to have to be

Further Reduction

patient and stay out of trouble."

"I'm laying as low as I can now," Adam replied, "Some of them are getting a little suspicious, I think."

"Why is that?" Jenny asked.

Adam reached into his bag and produced the dusty old Bible.

"I've been keeping to myself a lot more. Reading this." He laid the book on the coffee table.

"A Bible?" Jenny looked surprised and a bit confused. James just smiled.

"Where did you get a Bible, son?"

Adam snickered, "That's the one your friend tossed in my lap when he left me there in the church."

"What do you mean? I thought he let you go," Jenny said, "Did he leave you tied up in there?"

"I told him I would get out and he said he had to go. That he was running short on time and had to leave. I asked him if he was going to untie me and he said no, but that this should keep me company until I got loose. He said he just didn't trust me enough to not do something stupid."

James cackled out loud; a deep belly laugh that proved infectious to Adam as well.

"I can't say that I blame him, though," Adam continued, "If he hadn't left me there like that I probably *would* have done something pretty stupid."

"So, how did you get loose?" Jenny asked.

"You remember when you took me to see that first Avengers movie? It's been years ago, but I begged and pleaded to go see it in the theater."

"I remember."

"Well, there was the scene at the first where Black Widow is tied to a chair, right? And she has to fight all these guys so she can go and get the Hulk."

"Oh, you didn't," James said, the smile still broad on his face.

"Yeah, I did," Robinson continued, "I tried to flip the chair like she did and break it apart. It seemed like a good idea at the time."

Jenny began to laugh at the image of him

trying to maneuver himself like the crimson haired assassin.

"Didn't work, did it?" James asked.

"Well, I guess Russian wood isn't as sturdy as what we have around here," he laughed, "All I managed to do was fall over on the floor and dump the Bible out of my lap.

"It did loosen the ties enough that I was able to wriggle out, but that old chair is still in one piece.

"The funny thing about it is, well, as I was laying on the floor, trying to get myself free, I looked over at the Bible. The street lights were shining in on where I was and the Bible was a couple of feet away, so I couldn't see everything, but it had opened,"

Adam began to flip through the pages of the book, finally settling on Psalm 34.

"Depart from evil, and do good; seek peace and pursue it. The eyes of the Lord are upon the righteous, and his ears are open to their cry. The face of the Lord is against them that do evil, to cut off the remembrance of them from the earth."

Adam looked up at his aunt and uncle. A silence had fallen over the trio.

"It just, kind of, hit me; while I was laying there in the floor of the church. A man, a stranger I never met before, had just made me choose between life and death," he glanced back down at the Bible, "He tossed this in my lap, and all I could see in the gloomy glow of that street light was this passage. I knew I was doing wrong. He knew I was doing wrong. You did too. I just didn't want to admit it.

"I thought all I needed was money and power and cool cars. Big guns and girls and all the trouble I could take," He shook his head as he looked back at the table, "That don't mean nuthin.' None of it means nuthin' to me any more. I just want to get back where I used to be. Where I belong."

Jenny moved to her nephew's side and draped her arm across his shoulders, "It's OK, baby. We want you back too. We'll figure something out."

"Well, I have to admit, I like that man's style. Not only has he saved my boy's life, he got you on the path to righteousness to boot!" James smiled and laughed.

"James! That man's nothing but a criminal. He's no better than the men that Adam has fallen in with. I still think we should call the police." Jenny was still clearly agitated.

"Sometimes you have to break the rules to do what's right, Jenny. I know you don't understand that, but I do. I've had to break enough of them in my life, and he's trying to do the right thing," Carver said, trying to ease his wife, "Besides, even you can't argue with the results." He motioned to Adam who sat smiling as his aunt rested on the armrest of the chair.

"Hey, I gotta get goin.' Somebody will start askin' questions if I'm gone too long by myself. We ain't supposed to be out without a partner."

"Alright, son, alright. Go out the back if you need to," James said as he stood.

Adam dropped the Bible back in his bag and shook his uncle's hand, then hugged his aunt tightly.

"Come back in a few days and we'll see what we can come up with," Carver said, "I have a couple of ideas I need to talk to your aunt about."

Jenny escorted Adam to the back door. He quickly glanced across the yard and confirmed that nobody was looking before giving his aunt a final hug and stepping outside.

"Thank you. Thank you both," he stepped onto the top step, "I love you."

"We love you too. Go on, now. And be careful."

Chapter 16

Mark Himes strolled casually along the western edge of Carson Park, trying not to look out of place, but still making careful observations of everything he saw around him. Bends in the walking paths, thickets and bushes, tall trees with dense canopies, anything and everything he could see that would either help or hinder his line of sight.

Mark had stumbled on a peculiarity in the case. The rapist had struck three times so far. Each time it seemed to be random and unpredictable. As Mark studied the maps and information given to him by Thompson, he began to realize that the attacks took place every 27 days. Not once a month, not every thirty days, and not on a specific date, but every 27 days. While he couldn't explain the rationale, he couldn't deny the pattern.

He also noticed that each attack moved farther south in the park. Again, Mark couldn't explain the logic behind the movement other than to avoid striking in a location that might be under surveillance. Perhaps it was just that simple. Or, perhaps there was a psychological reason for the southward direction. That wasn't Mark's area of expertise, so he would let the professionals diagnose it.

He paused for a minute, looking back into the park and saw the bend in the sidewalk across the way he'd been looking for. A thicket of dense shrubbery obscured the visibility from the trail and would provide an opportune location for anyone with bad intentions.

Turning toward the buildings directly behind him, he saw a trio of old apartments with what appeared to be a good view of the concerning area. One still had a small store operating out of the main floor level. The other two seemed devoid of life. One actually had caution tape strung across the front door and plywood over the large windows at street level.

Himes quickly made his way across the street to the sidewalk for a closer look at the structures. As he stepped onto the concrete he noticed a uniformed officer just a few yards away heading his direction. John had told him they had stepped up patrols in the area due to the attacks and he had, in fact, seen a few other officers in the park itself already that day.

He pulled out his notepad and began jotting down the addresses of the buildings and noting their position relative to the point in the park he had observed. As he tucked the notepad into his shirt pocket a voice called out to him.

"Mr. Himes?"

Mark turned and saw the officer had closed to within a couple of yards. He could clearly see that it was Frank Carlisle, one of the officers he had met in John's precinct.

"Officer Carlisle! I didn't expect to see you here. What are you doing on this side of town?"

"Transferred. I grew up around here so someone thought it would be a good idea for me to work this side of town for a bit."

"Well, that makes sense, I suppose."

"What about you? What brings you to the

neighborhood?"

"Actually, I'm just being nosy," Mark said with a smile, "John told me about the problems over here recently and I love a mystery, so I thought I'd check it out. Who knows, maybe I might see something to help you guys catch him."

Carlisle smiled, "You never know. I know we've been working this area hard and haven't caught a break yet. Maybe a fresh perspective is what we need."

"So, Officer, how long have you been assigned here? I couldn't tell you when I last saw you at the station."

"About three and a half weeks and, please, call me Frank. You just got lucky to see me here at all," he smiled, "This is my short week."

Carlisle was referring to the typical work schedule where an officer would work twelve hour shifts for three days and then be off for four, then reverse the schedule the following week.

"I don't mind the transfer much, really. Like I said, I grew up a couple of blocks over, so I know the area pretty well. I used to know it better, but all this new construction and development has changed it a lot."

"I'll bet it has," Mark said, still studying the area.

Carlisle gestured to one of the buildings on Mark's list, "My grandmother used to live here. I can remember coming over and spending the night several times when my parents both had to work nights. We'd go down to the little Chinese place on the corner there and eat dinner pretty often.

"Now I hear that both of these are slated for demolition. Some new development is supposed to be in the works."

"Really? So, nobody lives here?"

"Only winos and junkies. We have to run them out pretty regularly. They come in and pass out a lot of times where they can have some privacy. It's kind of sad, actually."

Mark considered the locations even more seriously after hearing that.

"Now, I see that this one is boarded up and I assume the door is locked on that one. How do they keep getting in?"

"Different ways. Some will force the doors open, sometimes they crawl in through a loose window board. This one here has some windows out around back. We've told the owner to secure it several times, but he hasn't done anything yet."

"I guess it's cheaper not to do anything. No sense in putting more money into a building that's about to be torn down."

"I guess. It sure would make our jobs easier, though. Well, Mr. Himes, I guess I'd better get on the march. It's good to see you."

"Good to see you too. And don't call me Mr. Himes. It makes me feel old," Mark smiled.

"Well, no offense meant, but you probably are old enough to be my dad, you know," Carlisle grinned.

"Yeah, yeah, rub it in," Himes smiled, "Be careful out there."

Carlisle continued on the sidewalk, regularly scanning the park and alleys for anything that might be out of place.

Mark decided he would come back early in the morning and stake out the buildings to see if they actually could provide the view he needed. In the meantime he needed to call John.

Mark told Angie that he would be going in early most of the week to work on a ductwork problem at the station. Since there weren't as many people there in the early morning hours, he could get more done without being under foot. He hated to lie to his wife, but she could never know what he was actually doing. Despite the years of marriage and strong communication they had with one another, Mark wasn't sure how she would take knowing that he did what he did.

At around 3:00 in the morning, Mark arrived at the old apartment buildings. The building to the north was his first preference, so he scouted around back to see if he could find a way in. Peeking in through the windows with the night vision monocular he could, in fact, see a couple of people laying in rooms and hallways in various states of consciousness. The main floor was populated enough that he thought it might be best to look for another way in and turned his attention to the southern building.

The doors and windows all around the main floor were boarded up tight. Apparently the landlord had been by recently.

Mark stepped into the small alley at the side of the building and saw that the fire escape had been lowered. That either meant that someone had come down it or, even worse, someone else had gone up. Out of habit, Mark slid his hand over the grip to the 1911.

The morning was strangely quiet so he stood still and listened for any sounds emanating from within the old structure. After a few minutes of silence, he decided to try his luck at going to the roof.

The rusty iron framework creaked and complained as it took his weight, but it held. Mark decided to make it as quick a trip as possible for fear the assembly would fall under his mass. That was not an explanation he was prepared to give.

After several stealthy minutes of climbing, Himes finally stepped off the ladder to the roof. He scanned the vista with the monocular and saw no signs of occupancy on either structure. Carefully, he made his way across to the front of the building and laid down behind the façade, scanning the park in front of him. Through the glow of the street lights and trail lamps he could make out the thicket, but he couldn't see behind it. He needed to be on the other rooftop.

Gingerly he crept across, away from the street so he could eventually stand without worry of being seen by anyone below. He studied the space between the buildings and estimated the alleyway to be about eight feet wide. Not too far to jump, but it was still a four story drop to the ground.

"Come on, Mark," he mumbled to himself, *"You can do that with your eyes closed."* He stepped back a few paces and took a deep breath. Before over thinking the situation, he launched himself across the void and onto the other roof. He stumbled slightly, but was able to regain his footing and slip unceremoniously back to the side overlooking the park.

A quick scan of the area revealed the vantage he needed. If he was right, the spot he was looking at should be the location of the next attack and it should happen within the next four days. The 27th day would be the coming Friday.

Mark settled down and began to watch the park. He would stay there until just after dawn, then slip back down the adjacent fire escape and make his way back to the truck. He wasn't thrilled about being out with a rifle in the daytime, but in this instance, he didn't have much choice. The criminal dictated the terms of his crime and Mark had no input on it whatsoever.

While he was in recon mode, he decided to make full use of his time and began documenting the patterns of the police patrols in the area. As he suspected, they were very orderly and punctual. A true sign of a well disciplined force but, unfortunately, predictable as well. If the attacker had taken the time to observe, he would know when the best opportunity to strike would be also.

Just after sunrise, Himes noticed a pair of uniformed officers on what almost looked to be a leisurely stroll through the park. They had been through a couple of hours earlier, but this time something seemed to get their attention.

Within a few seconds, a young woman came jogging by, her long brown ponytail swaying from side to side with each step. The officers stepped to the side and let her have plenty of room to pass. She smiled and waved appreciatively as she continued on her way while the officers returned the salutation and admired her physique.

"*Not a clue,*" Mark grumbled.

After another hour, Himes began to make his way back to the fire escape. As he did, he decided to check the roof access door. A smile crept across his face as he got close enough to see that the knob and bolt had been long broken and the door itself was only lightly pulled to. He at least had a faster method down, though it might risk being spotted.

Mustering the courage to jump the alley again, Mark landed on the opposite side and swiftly began to descend to street level. He would be back the next morning to try it all again.

The next couple of mornings were rather

uneventful. Very little changed in the routines of the patrols and each morning it seemed that the same vagrants were inside the northern building. In fact, each morning, just after sunrise, the same brunette would come jogging down the winding concrete pathways through the park. She ran the same route every time and wore similar clothing each day, so Mark felt confident it was the same girl. She probably lived in the nicer apartments on the east side of the park and had no idea of the issues that had been going on there.

On Thursday Mark noticed one significant change in the location. Apparently, the police had made their routine stop to clean house at the northern building. When he peered through the windows that morning, not a soul was to be seen anywhere. He waited outside for a few minutes listening intently for any sounds inside. Satisfied nobody was conscious, he slipped through a window and into a small ground floor apartment.

Quietly he made his way from room to room until he came out in the front entry hall, near the old office. There were two stairways in the old building, one on the north end and one on the south. A hallway connected them with apartments on the east and west sides of the building. The apartments on the east faced the park while the west side had a lovely view of the alleys and crumbling buildings behind.

He made his way to the nearest stairway and began to climb. The old wooden steps creaked and popped with each step so badly that Mark wondered if it was worse to run up or sneak up. At least the sounds wouldn't linger at a more rapid pace. He began to step more toward the sides of the treads instead of in the middle. The logic being that the nails there might not have backed out as much over the years of foot traffic and so the noise might be lessened. It worked to an extent, but only just.

Floor by floor he inspected the building, finding no one else inside. That helped put his mind at ease a bit as he made for the narrow roof access steps. He pushed open the door at the top and scanned the area with his monocular. Seeing no signs of life he stepped out again onto the old roof and worked his way to the front of the building. After setting up his position like he had the night before, Mark settled in for another long, boring morning.

As he sat with his compact rifle on the rooftop, he could occasionally hear the faint chatter of police radio traffic below on the sidewalk. They would make rounds every hour and a half to two hours outside the park and every couple of hours inside. Timing the shot could be an issue if the pervert decided to strike at the wrong moment.

Just after sunrise, Mark spotted movement through the foliage. Right on time the woman appeared on the trail, ponytail bobbing. She again wore the same style clothes, traditional running shorts and a loose tank top with tennis shoes. Through a small opening in the branches he could see the officers on patrol heading the same direction she was. They stepped aside as she approached and let her pass, then fell back in line on their beat. It was just another day in the park.

But tomorrow was the 27th day.

Chapter 17

As Adam Robinson stepped around the corner of the house and into the darkness of the back yard he was greeted by an old familiar voice.

"Hello, son. Been wondering when you'd stop by."

Robinson jumped a little at the sudden soft voice in the shadows.

"Hey, Uncle James. You scared the crap out of me. I figured you'd be out here, but I wasn't sure what time you got out to smoke these days."

The elder lit his cigar and had a nice long draw, fumigating the back porch with a thick fog of smoke.

"Come on up here. I need to talk to you for a bit," he said gesturing to a lawn chair beside him on the porch.

Robinson climbed the steps and perched himself in the old chair.

Following the dimmed glow of another

deep drag from his cigar, Carver asked, "You had any more thoughts about what we talked about?"

"Yeah, I've been thinking about it a lot. I know we have some people coming in soon, and I think it would be best for me to be out before that happens. I hear that things will be a lot tighter once they are involved."

"So, how do you plan on leaving? Where are you thinking about going? How are you going to get there? What will you do when you get there?"

"See," Robinson began, "That's where I need the help. I want to come back home, but I know that wouldn't work and it might put you in danger too.

"I don't have any good contacts outside of town and no skills to get me a job anywhere. Not any kind of legal work, anyway. What do I do?"

"Your aunt and I have been talking about cashing out some of our savings to get you out of town. We can set you up with a little money to get you on your feet, but you would need to have a job and make ends meet. We can't afford to pay

Further Reduction

your bills and ours at the same time."

"No, Uncle James, no. I can't do that. That's your money. You earned it. That's for you to retire on, not for me to spend up."

"Shut up, son, and let an old man speak," James insisted, "I'm not done yet."

He shifted his weight in the chair to face his nephew, not that he could actually see him, but more for effect.

"We also have some money that we set aside for you to use for college. We had hoped that you would take the chance to make something out of yourself and get out of this dead end neighborhood. We started it when you were born and, well, we never touched it. We added to it until you were old enough to enroll, but you never did. That is also several thousand dollars now, and it's all yours. It was always going to be. What you do with it is up to you."

Adam sat stunned in the darkness. If James could have seen his face, he would have been quite amused by Robinson's shocked expression.

"As for contacts," James continued, "I

have that covered. I called some friends of mine and I have you a job and an apartment lined up. You'll have to pay the bills. The work won't be easy and you'll be expected to live up to your end of the deal, but it's a start. I would like for you to enroll in some classes and get your life back on track to something better, but, like I said before, it's up to you. The tuition money was meant for that all along.

"The seed money we will get for you will cover your initial expenses of food and housing for a couple of months. After that, well, you'll have to handle things yourself."

Adam was speechless. He hadn't known what to expect from the two of them, but it certainly wasn't this much.

"Uncle James, I…I…I can't…," Robinson stammered, desperate for the words that eluded him.

"Can't say no," James interjected, "That's right. You can't. Now, there's a catch. Are you ready?"

"Uh, yeah," Robinson managed to finally

blurt out.

"Good," Carver sat back in the chair and inhaled another long draw from the cigar. His appearance in the dimness of the back yard was almost like that of an interrogator. He seemed at ease with what he was about to say, but confident that he would get the answers he expected as well. Adam had seen the pose before many times when he was in trouble as a youngster.

"I need to know everything you can tell me about this visit you all are expecting. Names, dates, locations, numbers, and anything else you can think of. I need it all."

Adam thought for a moment. Why would his uncle need to know about all that? Was he going to call the police in? That would not be a good idea.

"Uncle James, I don't know why you're asking, but if you are thinking about calling the police, well, I wouldn't. It would be bad. Real bad."

"Don't you worry about why I need to know. You just be satisfied that I need to know.

Write it down if you want to, but I need that information."

Adam thought about it for a minute and softly began to speak. He didn't want anyone to be able to overhear him spilling the beans about what was coming. If he was identified as a leak, they would kill him without hesitation.

"Okay, in about two weeks there is a plane coming in from somewhere with some guys on it. They have connections to some big league people and they are coming here to expand their territory. The city is in a good location for distribution of drugs and stuff all over the U.S. That's why they are interested.

"T, the leader of our gang, has talked with them a few times and agreed to meet and see if we can work together on this. He's looking at it as a way to grab power and turf from the smaller gangs and get us a cut of the money when things sell."

"How many people are coming in? What date and what airport?"

"I don't know all that, but I can probably find out."

"What kind of business are these guys in? Just drugs?"

"Nah, they got their fingers in everything; weapons, drugs, kidnapping, gambling, you name it."

"And, T, he doesn't mind all that?"

"He's all about money and power. He used to have some limits, you know? Things he wouldn't do. Lines he wouldn't cross. Now? He don't care no more."

James considered everything his nephew said carefully. The information was ok, but incomplete. He needed more to give to Himes, so he pressed a little harder.

"So, basically, you're saying that some bad guys are coming in by plane from somewhere, to an airport somewhere nearby at some date in the future to grow their illegal business with the help of your friends. Does that about sum it up?"

Adam dropped his head.

"Uncle James, I told you, I don't know details. I'll try to find out, OK?"

"You can't tell me a time frame? Surely

you must know when they are coming? You obviously need to be getting prepared to meet these fine folks. Isn't anyone putting out the fine china?"

"I don't know an exact date, okay? I do know it's within the next two weeks. I know we are supposed to send a car to meet them at the airport, but I don't know what airport."

Robinson thought about it for a few minutes. His mind raced with how to get the information and finally it clicked.

"I know how I can find out. One of my friends is supposed to be the driver for the pickup. He'll know where and when. He should be able to tell me how many because he will need to take a vehicle big enough to carry everybody."

"That's a start anyway. If you can get me a tail number for the plane or names for your visitors, that would be good too."

Adam nodded his head silently, "I'll see what I can do," he glanced around the yard and surrounding neighborhood, "I need to get going. I'll be back in a couple of days and tell you what I find out."

"I'll be here," Carver said inhaling the last of the tobacco, "Be careful, son. We love you."

"Love you too…and thanks. I owe you everything."

Adam knocked lightly on the back door of the Carver home, checking over his shoulder frequently to be sure nobody had followed him. After a few minutes of waiting he heard the sound of movement from inside and soon the curtain swayed as his aunt peered into the darkness of the evening.

She unlocked the deadbolt and swung the door open just enough for her nephew to come inside, then swiftly locked it back behind him and the pair moved quietly to the small living room.

There, in his recliner, sat James Carver. His trusty cane rested against the armrest of the chair as he listened to an oldies station on the radio across the room.

Robinson sat across from his uncle and laid his pack on the floor beside the chair. A light thump could be heard as the Bible inside came to rest on the carpeted floor.

"Hey, Uncle James."

"Good evening," The man said in his deep grumbling voice.

Jenny appeared in the room with a pair of glasses of milk and began the task of distributing them.

"Hear any good stories lately?"

Adam shifted his weight in the chair and looked at the pair of elders before speaking.

"Yeah. Yeah I have," he began, "I talked to my friend, Bones, the driver for this meeting. He said that there were supposed to be five people coming in that he would be picking up at the airport. I don't know how many total are coming in, but only five are coming here. The pilot and crew or whatever may stay with the plane.

"He didn't know a tail number or anything, but he told me the names of the guys he's supposed to pick up; Kedzierski, Maskadov, Shishani, Rodriguez, and Dominguez. He wasn't told first names."

James studied the names for a minute. Finally he said, "Well, those don't sound like regular South American cartel names to me. Where are they coming from?"

"Two of them are from either South America or Mexico, I don't know which. The other three are Eastern European. Maybe Russian or something. They are all flying in together from either California or Nevada."

James nodded his head in agreement. The names did have a bit of a Russian sound to them.

"What airport?"

"McClendon Field. It's a little regional strip a few miles out of town. I've never been there, so I don't know where it is, really."

"That's alright, son, I know where it is," James said, "Any news on the time frame?"

"Yeah, Bones said he was supposed to take two cars up there on the 24th at 8:00 in the morning. The plane is supposed to come in some time between 8:00 and 10:00. One car is for picking them up and the other is for security."

"Are you in either group?"

"Nah," Robinson said, "'I said he wants me here to keep the patrols tight. He's worried about someone hittin' us here while he's out."

"He's not going to be here?"

"He's leaving with the group for the airport. Somethin' about makin' a good impression and talkin' business on the way back."

James considered all the information his nephew had presented to him. He would call the police contact in the morning.

"Where do you have your patrols running, Adam?"

Robinson began to outline the areas of town his patrols typically covered, and it was a large region. The patrols rotated every two hours, but how they ran their grid was up to each patrol.

One two-man team would most likely move in a different sequence through the streets than the next, making their predictability difficult at best. The closer to the theater they worked, the thicker the teams got. They had also recently begun using a drone for extra coverage, but it was still being tried out, so it wasn't used often.

Due to the recent loss of some members, they had begun running routine checks in some of the buildings as well. The school was inspected regularly as were the buildings to the south of the theater.

About once a night the old church would be checked out, but since nobody was aware of Robinson's experience there, they didn't look at it too hard. The neighborhood locations where Billy and the other two had been killed, close to the parking garage, were on the outer fringes, but were still patrolled a couple of times a day. Often it was a drive through check since nobody wanted to walk that far and it was a good distance from the safety and security of the theater.

When Robinson had finished he looked around at his aunt and uncle, waiting for the next question. They just stared blankly ahead, digesting the information, but unsure what to really make of it.

Finally Jenny cleared her throat and began to speak on a different subject.

"We called the bank the other day. It is going to take a few days to get the money out of the accounts, but we'll get it soon. You know how banks can be, they don't mind investing it for you in one of their IRA's or something, but they aren't very speedy about giving it back."

"We'll get it for you, son," James said, "but it might not happen before the 24th. They are dragging their feet a bit. I think they're afraid of losing one of their accounts with the economy so bad and all.

"Anyway, will that be alright if we can't time it out beforehand?"

"Yeah," Robinson said, a pang of regret carried in his voice, "You really shouldn't be digging into your savings for me. I feel bad that my decisions are what got me here."

"Yes, they did," Jenny said, "But you're our family, Adam. And this is what families do for each other. They make the bad decisions go away and they start over if they have to."

"I can go ahead and get a little less cash out earlier, if that would help," James said.

"No, no. Don't do that. I'll be fine. I'll just

keep my head down and try to play it safe."

"Too bad you can't call in sick," James muttered, "We used to have a boy years ago at the plant and when he didn't want to work he'd slip off and put a couple of eye drops in his drink. Made him sick as a dog. He'd start sweating and running a fever like he was going to die. His stomach would start cramping up on him and he'd run off to the bathroom every few minutes. Finally, the foreman would get tired of it and send him down to Medical. They couldn't figure it out, so they'd send him home. The next day he'd be back, blaming it on something he ate. He never lost any vacation days because the company doctors would send him home," James laughed at the memory, "Sneaky little bastard did it for who knows how long before someone saw him and figured it out."

Robinson laughed at the idea of trying something like that to get out of patrolling that day. It wouldn't work and he knew it. Still, he had to come up with something to keep him out of the fight that was coming.

Chapter 18

It was still an hour until the sun broke over the eastern horizon when she shut the engine off and began to pull her long brown hair back into a ponytail for her morning run.

There was a crisp coolness to the air with a tiny hint of humidity, but otherwise it was supposed to be a beautiful day. She slipped her MP3 player into the pouch on her left bicep and connected her headset as she reached for the door of her silver Honda Accord.

As she stepped out of the vehicle a rash of tiny chill bumps raced up both legs from the cool morning air and they continued to her back and shoulders. The running shorts and tee shirt didn't serve well as an insulating ensemble, but after her jog they would be excellent for managing the increase in body heat that came with vigorous exercise.

She closed the door on the car and stepped

over to a nearby bench to begin some light stretches and loosen up. It was a hard learned lesson from years earlier to always prepare before exercising. She didn't like the thought of having to endure torn or strained muscles again, so taking the extra time didn't bother her as much as it used to.

After a few minutes of limbering up she double checked her shoe laces and tightened them a little more, pulling the ankle high socks up just a bit as she did so.

Two uniformed officers strolled into view before she finished. It wasn't the same pair as the day before, but they were apparently on the same schedule as the others. She would see them a couple more times before her routine was finished.

"Good morning," one of them said with a small wave.

"Good morning," she replied with a smile.

That would be enough social interaction for now. She didn't come for conversation or for socializing. This was her respite from the world and a chance to prepare for the challenges of the day.

Not that she was rude, of course. Most people found her to be rather pleasant with a very likable disposition. But when she set her mind to something, she could be a bit singular of purpose. A one track mind as her mother used to say.

The officers casually walked around the bend in the trail and out of sight. She couldn't even hear their conversation anymore. It was time to get going. Before long the sun would be up and the park would begin to fill with all the patrons of the day.

Mothers with children packed for play dates and old men bound for the concrete tables where they would soon battle on the chess and checker boards would soon be there. The old women who seemed to have nothing but time and birdseed and a passion for pigeons would occupy her warm up bench.

After sunrise the other joggers would begin to arrive and the dog walkers would come with them. The park became a very busy place and stayed that way most every day. This was the best time to come, she thought.

The police had increased their presence recently and that had helped a lot with keeping the vagrants and drunks out, but sometimes the officers themselves could get in the way of a good run. They busied themselves with conversation and didn't pay attention to her swift approaches from time to time so she would need to go around them or slow down. It was a small price to pay for the extra safety and order that came with their company.

She began her run at a slow pace and gradually built up to a good jog. By her estimation, each trip around the park was roughly a mile, so she would take her first lap easily, then step it up for the second. Her third would be a cool down lap. If she was particularly stressed, she might take a fourth lap, but that seemed a bit out of the question today.

Soon after she began her run she passed the officers who still leisurely strolled the trails. She always assumed they were probably talking about her after she passed. After all, she was the only other person in the park on most days and even she, with all her modesty, would have to admit she looked pretty good. Of course, they could also be talking about how crazy she was for getting out this early every day to run. It really didn't matter to her one way or another. She simply turned the volume up on her playlist and carried on her way.

About a quarter of the way through the first lap, she crossed a pedestrian bridge over a small stream that fed the lake on the western half of the park. On the rail of the bridge leaned a man. She had seen him there before. He appeared to be feeding the fish below, but he always did it from the rail of the same bridge. He would lean against the rail almost as if he were contemplating jumping. He never said a word to her as she passed and never made an effort to get out of her way. He just stood there, dropping little chunks of crackers or bread into the water below.

Without slowing her pace she stepped to the right side of the bridge and passed the man in silence. The only sound was that of her hot pink shoes slapping the deck of the bridge. Soon she was back on ground level and around the bend under the canopy of the huge oak and maple trees that grew throughout the area.

Before long she reached the champion tree at the halfway point; a massive old oak that stood majestically on the southern end of the park. She always wondered how old the tree was. Judging by the trunk diameter it must have been hundreds of years old.

"If you could only talk," she said quietly to herself as she rounded the bend, wondering what stories it could tell if it were able to speak.

Up ahead she thought she saw someone cross the trail. It was difficult to be sure because it was rather fast movement. It could have just been the breeze playing with the branches of the low lying junipers. The yellowish light emitted from the trail lamps didn't lend well to visibility either, but they did make the park an almost romantic locale. She often thought it might look like the woods of Narnia from the book series by C.S. Lewis.

As she got closer to the spot she looked to

where she had seen the movement and spotted a stray dog sniffing around some swings. There was the culprit. She had seen him around the park before as well. He had a collar, but she never had been close enough to see what it said. She hated the idea of Animal Control being called to pick him up, but there was little she could do to help him find home either. She certainly couldn't carry him home with her; the apartment manager would have a coronary. Thankfully, the officers in the park hadn't bothered to call him in. Perhaps they didn't like the idea of him going to the pound either.

Within a few minutes she was passing the bench where she had warmed up. Lap two had begun.

She paused for a minute to check her pulse rate and time before continuing on down the trail. The little monitor she wore on her wrist would keep track of all the steps she took and calories she had burned as well as a plethora of other fitness and health data. It had made a world of difference in the way she ate and exercised

Further Reduction

With her warm-up lap out of the way, it was time to get serious. She began lap two at a much more brisk pace and soon was in a full run. She couldn't maintain the entire route at that speed, but she would do most of the trail that way; occasionally slowing down to catch her breath or step around the man on the bridge, or the police, or the dog.

Once again she found herself at the giant oak tree and she slowed her pace for a bit. After only a few seconds of rejuvenation, she pressed on with the sound of classic Guns and Roses pounding in her ears. Up ahead she saw the dog frantically sniffing the ground and pacing back and forth. He usually found a squirrel or two to antagonize every morning and looked to be hot on the trail of one.

The sky had begun to lighten ever so slightly as the sun was beginning to break. She could already hear the waking birds begin to sing. The officers appeared on the trail ahead, not terribly far from where she had first passed them.

Coming up from behind she noticed one

of them glance back in her direction and motion to the other to make room. Like a parting curtain the blue uniforms split, exposing the concrete pathway between. She smiled as she passed between the two and began lap three.

On the cool down lap she preferred to jog about halfway and walk in the last half. It was a slower, more comfortable approach, but she enjoyed it. The timing was nearly perfect as well.

When she reached the oak for the third time, she slowed her pace to a walk and turned down her music. She scrolled through the playlist and selected some slower tempo tunes to accompany the walk.

She could see the dog, still on the trail of whatever he had been after earlier. He sniffed in silence all around the merry go round and swings before stopping to use a large sugar maple for a urinal. Quietly he disappeared behind the bushes at the bend in the trail.

As she got closer to the thicket, she could hear the dog rummaging and stirring inside the bush. This was as close as she had ever been to him. Maybe she could even see the name on the collar and get the owner to come and pick him up.

She slowed to peer into the underbrush. Unable to see the canine, she moved around to the back side of the bushes for a better angle. Suddenly, the foliage erupted beside her as a hand clasped across her face and drug her into the shadowy realm off the trail.

He pulled her through the shrubbery and into a small opening beyond. Still behind her, she couldn't see what the man looked like, but she could tell he was considerably larger and stronger than she was.

She felt his free hand begin to slide up her thigh and tug on her running shorts, trying to free them from her waist.

Thinking quickly she raised her right foot and pressed the inside of her hot pink Nike against his left calf muscle. Driving down and in at the same time unleashed a torrent of pain across the man's leg and he grunted loudly, almost yelling from the sudden removal of skin and hair.

She drove the heel of her foot hard into

the top of his, again sending shards of pain through the man's senses, but he still held on. He had stopped fumbling at her clothes, but had tightened his grip on her mouth. She began to worry that he might break her neck and then have his way with her limp body anyway.

She pulled her arm forward and slammed her right elbow back, driving it into his chest as hard as she could. The man gasped for breath and loosened his grip enough that she was able to turn and face him.

He was probably six feet tall or more, a giant compared to her five foot five inch frame and he clearly outweighed her by at least 100 pounds. Still, the fight of her life was on and she wasn't giving up that easily.

Still determined to finish what he started, the man grabbed with one hand and punched with the other, his greasy, all too black hair hanging before his eyes. If he couldn't catch her and get her to cooperate, he'd simply knock her out and finish the task.

She side stepped each advance while reaching up under her shirt. The sudden move to her own chest confused him and he slowed for just a second to try and make sense of what she was doing. Would she be a willing party to his perversion?

The miniscule delay on his part was all she needed to securely grip and draw the small Glock 43 handgun from its hiding place. She jammed the muzzle into his chest, angling upward from her smaller vantage and quickly pressed the trigger twice.

A pair of nine millimeter hollow points punctured the man's shirt and raced upward through the chest cavity, tearing tissue in the lungs as they expanded. A look of confused desperation came across the man's face as he lunged for her again.

A third shot slammed into the attacker from under his left arm, the round obliterating the left lung and heart. He dropped to the ground without another sound.

She stood for what seemed like several minutes gazing at the man who had only moments before had her at his command. A patch of crimson began to saturate the camouflaged tee shirt he wore, appearing as an almost black stain in the early morning light. Then it dawned on her; where did the third shot come from?

She panned the area, looking for a policeman, but none were to be seen. She looked at her own pistol. Had she fired the third shot? No. She hadn't. She quickly snapped the handgun back into the holster and ducked from the thicket, scanning the area carefully again before collecting the spent casings and running to the nearest wall of the park.

Quickly and quietly she made her way back to the Honda. From the sidewalk outside the park she could see the two officers running toward the south, no doubt coming to her rescue after hearing the gunfire. The radio chatter faded as she opened her car door and got inside.

With no time to think, she started the engine and left as casually as the adrenaline would allow.

Chapter 19

Mark arrived at the apartment house about 3:30 in the morning. He quietly made his way to the rear entrance of the building and peeked inside. To his dismay, there sat a man on the floor of the hallway, an empty whiskey bottle just out of his grip.

"Seriously?" Mark's frustration had begun to mount. He had hoped that the drunks and dope heads would have stayed out of the building one more night so he could get this job done without complications. He had no choice but to go next door and climb the rickety old fire escape again.

He cautiously navigated the rungs of the ladder, negotiating with a quiet commentary that it hold together just for one more day. After that it could fall into dust for all he cared.

Finally he reached the top and stepped clear of the rusty old death trap. Now came his favorite part of the journey: jumping the alley between the buildings.

He slipped quietly up toward the front of the building and listened momentarily for any sounds on the street below. The last thing he needed was someone to see him soaring like an albatross between the structures. Well, perhaps an albatross was too elegant for him. More like an emu shot from a canon.

He said a few words of encouragement to himself under his breath and began to run toward the alley. With a great push he launched himself toward the other building, clearing the gap with room to spare. The landing, however, would not have earned an Olympic gold metal by any stretch of the imagination.

He landed on his right foot and gauchely fell as the mass of the duffel bag came down on his back. With a slight roll he came to rest a few feet from the edge of the building.

"Oh, that sucks," Himes mumbled to himself. The pain in his ankle was already beginning to grow. After a quick examination he determined that nothing was broken, but it certainly was twisted. He gathered his bag up and listened again for any indication that he had been heard. With only silence meeting his ears he looked the roof over and began to carefully make his way to the front edge of the building.

Trying to ignore the pain, he set up his rifle and dug the monocular out of his pocket. It wouldn't do much good from this distance, but he might be able to see something if it were close enough.

As he sat there, peering over the façade, he could hear the approaching officer on the sidewalk below. The radio crackled with unintelligible traffic every few seconds. As the man came into view Himes watched. He never looked up, but was constantly watching the park and the buildings beside him.

From time to time a vehicle would pass through, but none stopped. Rarely one would be a patrol car. Himes began to wonder if John had mentioned the timing and location changes to the chief. Perhaps there were extra officers covering the area tonight because of his own reconnaissance.

After a long, uneventful first hour or so, Mark noticed a car on the far side of the park that appeared, through the trees, to be slowing down as if to stop. He couldn't see anything beyond headlights and tail lights as the vehicle pulled into a parking place toward the north end of the park, but he was relatively sure it had stopped. He checked his watch. That would probably be the jogger he had seen so regularly on his stake outs.

His thoughts switched to the young lady and he wondered why nobody had told her to stay clear of the park. It seemed terribly negligent on the part of the police to allow her to continue to come and run every day when they had had the attacks. Maybe they thought the situation was under control since there hadn't been any recently. Maybe they were right. Maybe they had told her to stay away and she was one of those adamant people that would always demand that she had the right to be there. True, but not always an intelligent argument.

Maybe she was actually a cop. Now, that

made more sense. She could be working for the police department to set up a sting and catch the guy. That thought made Mark stop and think. If that were the case, why hadn't John said anything? Surely he would know if an undercover operation had been started around a case he had given Himes. If she was an undercover officer, what would happen if he pulled the trigger and took the perpetrator out?

All the thinking was becoming a distraction. Himes decided to clear his mind and focus on the job. If the girl was an officer, he'd let her do her job. If she was unable to, he would take the shot and let things fall where they would. He secretly kind of hoped that she was a cop, because he really didn't feel like running to the truck with his ankle throbbing the way it was.

He put the monocular back to his eye and began to watch the trails across the street as much as he could. Within a few minutes the girl appeared from under the canopy and into an opening along the western edge of the park.

She jogged leisurely along, her ponytail

bobbing back and forth like a metronome. He could make out the MP3 player on her bicep, but through the grainy resolution of the night vision device he couldn't see details like the headset or cord from this distance. The angle of the vantage also prevented a clear picture of her face.

Another disadvantage of the night vision was that everything was shaded in a green monochrome wash. He could see features, but not color. He had considered spending the extra money on a better device, but had a hard time convincing himself of it being worthwhile. John had suggested trying to find one of the old Sony Cyber Shot cameras that could see through some dark clothes since it would help expose weapons on suspects, but Mark had decided against it. There were some things he just simply didn't want to see.

He would simply have to make do with what he had available. The sun would be up before long anyway and he would put the device back in his pocket until the next time he needed it.

Across the street came the patrol. The two officers chatted about something as they walked around the park trails checking the dark corners and thick bushes along the way. A stray dog wandered into view shortly afterward, sniffing around the swing set toward the far side.

Mark watched the dog for a few minutes to see if it reacted to anything nearby since it was very close to the spot he was most concerned about. So far the only movement he'd noticed was the canine.

Soon the girl appeared to his right. She was approaching the thicket he suspected. He moved closer to the rifle, but knew if he had to take a shot now it would literally be a shot in the dark. The illumination provided by the little street lamps throughout the park wasn't enough to accurately shoot by. He needed to wait for sunrise. Hopefully, the suspect would too.

The girl passed by without incident and a few minutes later the police patrol sauntered by as well. Neither seemed to bother the dog who apparently had found something very interesting to track.

The girl came by on her second lap of the

morning and was in a flat out run this time. Soon she was across the opening in the trees and out of sight again. She would typically make three to four laps each morning, so Mark knew she was around her halfway point. He shifted his attention back to the other side of the park.

He thought he saw movement, but it was still too dim to be sure and it was too far for the monocular to be effective. It could have been the dog again, but Himes wasn't sure. He began to watch the area closer.

Soon the girl blasted by once again, on her way to finish the second lap of the morning. If she was true to her routine, she would have at least one more lap before leaving the park.

As the sun began to rise he put the monocular away and settled in behind the rifle scope. The view was much better now and he could see details that were absent through the green glow of the night vision.

The girl passed by on the near side of the park once more. This time she was at a considerably slower pace. Himes guessed she would be going home after this lap since she was apparently winding down.

He dialed up the magnification and zoomed in on the far side of the park a little. He didn't want to develop tunnel vision, so he kept the field of view wide enough to see the area around the thicket that had his concern. To the left he could see the dog still around the playground equipment.

The Sheppard mix sniffed his way over to a large sugar maple and promptly urinated on it before heading toward the bushes. Something new got his attention and he turned left behind the shrubbery and headed across the street. Seconds later the girl came into view.

Himes watched her as she approached the bushes. What was she doing? Looking for the dog? She stooped over and peered into the thick branches of the bush, seemingly reacting to something within.

Suddenly a man burst forth from the foliage and wrapped his hand across the young woman's face, dragging her through the hedge to the opening behind.

Mark flipped the safety off and increased the magnification on the optic, but he simply couldn't see through the branches well enough to take a shot. He could clearly see the color of her tee shirt and hot pink shoes, but the man remained blurry and indistinct.

Without warning, the man stumbled backward into the opening that Mark had hoped to utilize, the girl still firmly within his grasp. The shot was compromised.

"Come on, girl, get away from him so I can drop him," Mark said under his breath.

She scraped his inner leg with her foot and then stomped his foot hard, but he still held. Finally, she drove her elbow back, knocking the breath out of him. The man relented and dropped his hold.

"Atta girl!" Mark whispered as he gripped the rifle and began to press the trigger. Then he saw her do something unexpected. She reached up under her shirt, almost as if she was unhooking her bra.

"*What are you doing?*" Mark thought. Clearly the attacker was confused as well.

The man lunged forward and she met him with an upper cut to his chest. Mark decided to take the shot. He might not get another chance.

As he pressed the trigger he could swear he heard a pair of muted pops. Through his scope he could see the shocked expression on the man's face as he dropped to the ground. In her hand the young lady held a pistol; a nine millimeter Glock, by the looks of it. She glanced at the body and then looked at her hand, unsure of the results before her. She quickly shoved the pistol back under her shirt and stepped to the edge of the clearing, looking left and right before stepping out. Quickly she collected the pair of brass shell casings and gripped them deep in the palm of her hand.

As she stepped through the opening she scanned the area before her again, probably looking for the police, or whoever had taken the third shot. As she looked in his direction, Himes focused on her as tightly as he could.

"What the…"

Police radio chatter on the street below told him it was time to move. Apparently an officer had been close enough to the building to hear the shot and was now coming to investigate. He took his eyes off the scope as the girl quickly headed out of the park and turned north to her car.

Himes broke the rifle down, shoved it into the bag and began to low crawl across the roof to the access door. His ankle throbbed at the sudden application of pressure and movement. Maybe he should put together an emergency kit for things like this. He'd worry about that later.

He made it to the stairs and quickly got to the upper floor, but he could already hear the echo of a police radio coming from below.

The officer was calling in shots fired from inside the building and was working to clear the structure alone, apparently. Amid his calls for backup Mark could hear other officers, presumably the pair in the park, also calling for backup and shots fired there.

Mark's mind raced as he tried to come up

with a plan to escape. He certainly couldn't outrun anyone with his ankle twisted the way it was. What were his other options?

He glanced up and down the hallway. Nothing came to mind, so he began to make his way toward the southern stairwell. The radio chatter seemed to be louder toward the northern end.

He surprised himself at how quickly he managed to get to the next floor below with as little noise as he made, but he wasn't out yet. He could hear the radio one floor below his location and it was on the move. He glanced across the hallway and saw an array of whiskey bottles, some empty, some partially filled. An idea struck him. It had to work.

Himes dropped his duffel bag against the baseboard beside the bottles and sat down against it, using the bag as a back rest. He stretched his legs out in front of him and grabbed one of the partial bottles, proceeding to pour it on his shirt and pants.

It smelled awful. It smelled like…urine.

Himes held the container up to his nose

and took a cautious sniff.

"Dammit!" He tossed the bottle down the hallway, slapping it against the wall as it slid to a sudden stop. Then he had an epiphany.

"Hey!" he yelled, "Come back here!"

Moments later a uniformed officer appeared at the north stairwell with his weapon drawn. Himes lowered his chin to his chest and pretended to be hopelessly intoxicated.

The officer approached him slowly; his radio microphone in his left hand.

"Dispatch this is 509 I have a suspect on the move in the apartment building. Possible witness. Please stand by."

"Copy 509. Dispatch standing by," came the response.

"Hey," the officer nudged Mark's foot, "Hey, did you see anyone up here today?"

Channeling his best Foster Brooks impression, Himes rolled his head up slightly and addressed the policeman.

"Hey, ossifer. Hey, you need to catch that sumbish. He owes me a bottle."

"What did he look like? What was he wearing? Where did he go?"

"Aw, he was a great big bassard. Probly sebem foot or so. Wearin' a red shirt an' some britches an' carryin' a bazooka! He came runnin' down here from over there and kicked my bottle outta my hand. That sumbish owes me a bottle of Early Times!"

"Okay, which way did he go?"

"Go? Hell, I don't know. He ran to them steps, but I don't know where he went after that. Maybe he went to buy me a bottle of Early Times. He owes me one, you know."

"Yeah, you mentioned that. Look, you need to get out of here. This is private property for one thing and we have an armed man on the loose for another."

"But I was sleepin.' I'm awful tired, see?" Mark motioned for the officer to come closer. The man leaned in a little but the smell of Himes' disguise was already beginning to nauseate him.

"I'm also a little tipsy," Mark chuckled, "But don't tell nobody."

"Uh huh. I tell you what. You get your stuff and get out of here right now and I won't haul you in for public drunk and trespassing. Deal?'

"Ok, ok," Mark said as he began to shuffle around on the floor, trying to get up without giving himself away.

The officer headed down the steps and out of sight. Mark gathered his bag and limped to the opposite stairwell, gingerly making his way to the street level below.

When he stepped out, the neighborhood was thick with patrol cars and an ambulance could be seen through the trees on the opposite side of the park.

He fumbled through the scene and overheard the officer telling some others nearby that Himes was the only witness he'd found, but he was so drunk he had urinated all over himself and was, at best, unreliable.

Mark turned the corner and smiled to himself. For the time being he just had to go somewhere and clean up. Then he had some new business to take care of.

Chapter 20

Thompson's shift started at six in the morning. He had just managed to take his seat with the first of many coffee cups when his telephone rang. Trying not to still sound half asleep he answered.

"Detective Thompson. How can I help you?"

The voice on the other end was deep and authoritative, almost as if James Earl Jones had called.

"Mr. Thompson, my name is James Carver. We have a mutual friend."

John was now wide awake.

"Oh? And who would that be, Mr. Carver?"

"I don't know his name, but he gave me your number and said it would be the best way to get a message to him. That's why I'm calling. I need to speak to him. Urgently."

"Ok. What's the message? I'll pass it along as quickly as I can."

The phone sat silently for a second as Carver considered what to say.

"Just tell him I'm in the mood for pancakes; as soon as possible."

"Pancakes? That's the message?"

"Your friend seems like a smart man, Mr. Thompson. If he can't figure it out, I suspect what I have to say needs to be said to someone else. Thank you for your time."

"Hang on," Thompson began, but the line was already dead. Thompson sat for a minute and decided he needed some fresh air for the next call. He grabbed his burn phone and headed toward the sidewalk.

Mark was able to change into his spare clothes in the relative privacy of his truck, but even going commando as he was the odor of the bottle hung to his skin. He had disposed of the tainted clothing in a garbage dumpster near where he had parked, but the stench still lingered with him. It wasn't as bad as it originally was, mind you, but it was still bad. All he could think about was taking a shower with lots of soap and hot water.

As he made his way toward the house he had the windows rolled down to help ventilate the cab and almost didn't hear the phone over the road noise.

Glancing over at the device, he snapped it up and saw it was Thompson calling.

"Yeah?"

"Good morning, sunshine! Isn't it a lovely day?"

"No. It is a horrible day and I want to go home."

"Well, from all the buzz around here I'd say it has at least been an eventful morning. Wouldn't you agree?"

"Oh, it's been eventful, alright," Himes snapped. His ankle was absolutely pounding with pain as he tried to work the accelerator pedal.

"Well it isn't over yet, buddy. I just got a call from your friend Carver."

"Carver? What did he want?"

"Pancakes."

Himes sat silently for a minute.

"What? Pancakes? What's that supposed to mean?"

"He said to tell you that he was in the mood for pancakes as soon as possible. He also said you would know what that meant," Thompson gave him a second to think it over, "You do know what he means, don't you?"

"Ah, crap," Himes exclaimed, "Now? Like, right now?"

"ASAP."

"Son of a," Himes let the comment dangle, "Alright, but he won't have much of an appetite when I get there."

"Do I want to know?"

"Oh, you'll want to know, but I'm not telling you. You're going to have to wait to hear *this* one."

Thompson smiled into the phone. What had Mark gotten himself into this time?

"Well I just can't wait to see you, then."

"Trust me, you'd be a lot better off if you

did. Gotta go. Apparently I have to ruin someone's breakfast."

Mark pulled over and pointed the truck in the direction of Pancake Country. Soon he was parking outside the establishment and could see the Carvers through one of the large windows.

"I hope you have already eaten," he mumbled to himself as he got out of the vehicle and headed for the door.

As he stepped inside, the sudden chill of the room sent a shiver down his spine. He sat down at the bar that ran the length of the building on a stool nearest to the Carvers. Soon the waitress stepped up to take his order. She snurled her nose a bit as she managed a weak smile.

"Good mornin' honey. What can I get you?"

Mark smiled understandably at her somewhat warped facial expression, "I'll just have some coffee, please."

"One coffee. I'll be right back," she said as she quickly stepped away.

Himes twisted around in the seat, glancing

over at the Carvers who shared the same look as the woman behind the counter. Jenny had her napkin up covering her face while James just sat there with a foul appearance.

"Good morning," Mark said with a smile, "Sorry about the smell. It's a lot better than it was."

Jenny just nodded, giving the strange man a long look up and down and wondering what could make a person smell like that. James just grunted and cracked a tiny smile of his own.

Moments later the waitress appeared again and sat a steaming cup of coffee in front of Mark. He quickly doctored it with a little cream and sugar and began to sip at it enthusiastically.

From behind him he heard James begin to rustle in his seat.

"I need to go to the bathroom," he said to Jenny, "That coffee is making a quick trip this morning."

Mark quickly drank the rest of his own cup and made his way to the restroom as well. As he opened the door he scanned the room. Carver stood at the sink washing his hands and shaking his head from side to side with a smile on his face.

"Son," he said, almost laughing, "What in the hell have you gotten into? You don't smell like yourself today."

"It's a long story. I was on my way home to shower when I heard you wanted pancakes."

"You say you smell better now than before? I don't see how that's possible."

Mark grinned, "Oh, it's possible. You would have been able to smell me from the road before."

"Who says I didn't anyway?" the old man grinned back, "Listen, I don't want to take all your time because you really need to go and clean up. I did want to thank you for scaring the piss out of my nephew."

"You're welcome."

"He's still carrying that Bible you tossed in his lap and reading it every day. We've been trying to work on a way to get him out of that mess without him looking like a snitch."

Mark was surprised. He didn't expect the

young man to have a total change of heart like that. Well, so much the better.

"Hey, I was glad to help. I'm sure you will come up with something."

"We already have, but the problem is that we can't finish our plan until after you will have to deal with some things yourself."

Mark was confused now.

"How do you mean?"

"Jenny and I are going to get him set up with some cash and a job out of town. I've pulled some strings and he's all set but we can't get the money until after the 24th. Bankers and their paperwork, you know."

"OK, what's that got to do with me?"

"The 24th is when company is coming."

Mark began calculating the date and time he had to prepare. There was a lot to factor in and now his ankle was an issue to consider as well.

"Did he give you a time?"

"Eight o'clock in the morning at McClendon Field. Five guys plus maybe a flight crew with two drivers and a security team coming to pick them up. No first names, but the last names are Rodriguez, Dominguez, Shishani, Mazkadov, and Kedzierski.

"You're probably thinking the same thing I did: those don't all sound like names from south of the border do they?"

Himes' eyes opened wide at the information. There was no way he could handle all that alone. Not on the airport grounds, anyway. There were too many variables to consider; too many places to hide and too much property to be liable for.

If he waited until they all got back to the theater there would be reinforcements and that drone flying about on top of it all. There was no way he could channel them all in and pick them off as they entered the back door. Again, there were armored vehicles and buildings close by that provided ample cover and concealment. No good answer presented itself.

"Your nephew," Himes began, "Is he going to the airport?"

"No. He's supposed to stay at the theater

and run the patrols. He's trying to figure out how to get out of it."

"OK. If he can keep his head down and out of the way, he should be fine. I wasn't expecting all this," Mark's mind was racing with all the information, lost in options and not really finding any that would work.

"You got this?"

"I'll get it, one way or another. I just have to figure out how."

"OK, son. Go clean up. I gotta get back to my wife and get away from you. You stink. Make me want to toss my pancakes back up."

"Yeah," Mark smiled, "That'll teach you to call on a moment's notice."

Mark passed his seat, dropping some cash on the counter to cover his coffee and the inconvenience of his aroma then headed for the truck. It had finally come time for that shower he needed.

One of the benefits of living in the country the way the Himes' did was that you rarely got visitors you didn't expect. The remote location and long driveway were filters to keep most people from just dropping by unannounced. Their neighbors weren't far away, but they were distant enough that Mark felt completely comfortable stripping down outside and burning his clothes in the burn barrel beside his shop. There was no way he would bring them into the house.

He streaked casually across his back yard and straight to the bathroom where a long hot shower with lots and lots of soap awaited him.

After several minutes he appeared from the steam filled room feeling more than refreshed. He rummaged through the closet, selecting a casual, yet presentable ensemble and proceeded to get dressed.

Chapter 21

Mark pulled into a spot just down from Miranda's book store and walked up to the front door. There was still a faint odor in his truck, so he simply left the windows down a bit and hoped it hadn't gotten back on him.

He stepped inside and quietly made for the coffee and scones.

Miranda was addressing a pair of customers toward the back of the store as he entered. She glanced to the door and shot him a big smile as Mark turned toward the chairs at the front.

After a few minutes the customers thanked Miranda for her time and stepped out the door, heading for a convertible BMW parked directly out front. She helped herself to a cup of coffee and sat down across from Mark.

"Whew," she said with a smile, "Busy morning."

"Yeah," Mark replied, "I saw that."

"What brings you around this morning? Needing a new book or just wanting to set John up for another prank?" She sipped long at her cup, cutting her eyes across at Mark.

"Neither, actually. I wanted to talk to you about your fitness routine."

She sat her coffee down on the table and looked at Mark quizzically.

"My fitness routine? Ok. What do you want to know and I'll tell you all my secrets," she smiled again.

"Ever go jogging early in the morning?"

She shot him an odd look, trying to figure out where this was headed.

"Yes, I jog pretty regularly. Sometimes in the morning and sometimes in the evening when I leave here. Why? Are you looking for a running partner?"

"You ever been running in Carson Park?"

Miranda leaned back in her seat and stared at Mark's face intently.

"A few times. They have a nice trail, but John told me they were having some problems over there and to stay away. Why?"

"Because I saw you there."

Miranda sat in her seat, her mouth wide open as she scrambled for the words that eluded her.

"This morning, I saw you in the park."

Mark leaned back in the chair and took a long sip of the coffee, waiting to see how she would respond.

"You must be mistaken. Maybe you saw someone who looked like me."

"Oh, she looked *exactly* like you. I got a really good look, too."

"Really? How, um, how close were you, exactly?"

"I was about 425 yards away, but through the 50 mm objective lens on my Leupold scope, it might as well have been a couple of inches."

Miranda's expression softened.

"You're the third shot."

"I'm the third shot," Mark said, "and now you have me in a bit of a bind."

"What do you mean?"

"Well, see, I was there to eliminate a predator; an individual known to the police to have been attacking women in the area over the past several weeks. So, I did my homework and staked out the area for the past few days. The problem is that someone else showed up that I hadn't counted on: you."

Miranda said nothing but carefully studied Mark's face, trying to determine if he was still a friend or if their relationship had changed.

"I saw you shoot the man this morning. I shot him trying to save you, but you didn't need my help."

"Mark…I…"

"Just hang on a second. Let me finish," he scratched at his chin trying to formulate his thoughts carefully, "See, when I saw you kill him, I knew you were the one that had been shooting guys all year and leaving no traces. You are the vigilante that they've been looking for and can't find."

"I…,"she began again.

"No, just hang on," Mark said, carrying on

his explanation, "Since they have been having so much trouble, John asked me to take the job of eliminating the vigilante too."

Miranda's eyes grew as she stared at Mark. She couldn't think of what to say, but she was genuinely beginning to fear for her life.

"What am I supposed to do, Miranda? My job was to take you out because you are a loose canon, working outside the law. You have a price on your head and I have the contract for it."

"Does John know?"

"Nope. And I don't want to be the one to tell him either. The only way that I can see this working is if you stop doing what you're doing and I forget what I saw," Mark met her eyes across the table, "Will you stop?"

"Mark," she began, stumbling as she formed the sentences, "I can't. Do you want to know why?"

"Indulge me," Mark said, grasping for any fair reason not to have to turn her in or kill her.

"Did John tell you about what happened to me?"

"In a nutshell, yes."

"Well, I do what I do so that others don't have to go through what I did. There are a lot of sick people out there, Mark. You know that. You've seen it yourself. I don't want anyone to have to be put through what I was, so I stop it. I have to stop it because the system doesn't work."

Mark considered her opinion before saying a word.

"You're right; the system does have its flaws. A lot of times people get away with heinous things because they know how to exploit the system and walk from their crimes. But that doesn't give you the authority to be judge, jury and executioner. Even worse, you're deliberately setting people up to fall into your trap and *then* you play those roles."

"What about you?" she demanded, "Who authorized you? Who gave you the permission to go out and kill that man this morning? You're just like me. You find the bad guys in the world and you put them down to protect others."

"I'm not like you. For me it's business. I

don't get personally involved in it. I'm not on a mission to clean up the city for my personal satisfaction. I get a contract and I take the person out. Period. I don't trap them into doing something bad and then drop them. They're already doing bad things and I stop them…for a price. A price that's cheaper than taking them to jail and sending them to prison; that's simpler than having officers fill out tons of paperwork only to have a slick lawyer or a crooked judge let them off with a slap on the wrist and time served.

"My problem right now is not them; it's you. You're on my list and I need to know how to get you off it."

Both sat in silence, trying to figure out the resolution to the situation. Finally Miranda spoke up.

"I have a moral obligation to myself, to do what I do. To help those who can't get it through the legal avenues. I would think that you, of all people, would understand that. After all, you're the reason I do it."

Mark looked up at her, an expression of

confusion flashed across his face.

"When I had my...incident I felt terrible. I wanted to crawl into a hole and die. I couldn't face anyone. I couldn't live with the embarrassment and shame of what happened. But I took that and I turned it around. I decided to never let it happen to me again. So, I trained.

"I trained in Krav Maga, Brazilian Ju Jitsu and some other self defense forms. I took handgun courses and began to carry. I began to get in shape so I could fight back and protect myself.

"Then I saw you in the paper. I saw what you did in the restaurant that day and I knew that if you could stand up and fight for other people, so could I. I knew that being able to defend and protect myself was only part of what needed to happen; that I needed to protect others like me as well. That's when I decided to be 'pro-active' towards crime."

Mark measured her words thoroughly. He was frustrated and yet sympathetic. He couldn't kill her. That was out of the question. But, he couldn't turn her in. That would devastate John, not to mention Angie and the kids. They had all become fond of her. Even worse, she could identify Mark for the work he'd been doing as well. Still, she couldn't keep gunning people down at her own discretion. If Mark couldn't resolve the situation, his only choices would lead to painful complications. All except one.

"You won't stop, then?"

"I can't."

"Okay. I have a proposition for you, then."

Miranda sat up in the chair. Was he going to hand her over to the police? Maybe she could appeal to John's affections and he could get her some leniency. No, Mark wouldn't turn her in, would he?

"I'm listening."

"Work with me."

"Excuse me?"

"You won't stop being Miss Punisher, so will you rein it in and work with me to do the job under the oversight and control of the police department?"

She thought about it for a few seconds. If

she agreed, she would be at the mercy of the department to determine who needed to be dealt with. Her instinct was to not give up the control. That was one thing that made her such a good IT person. She knew what needed to be done and how to do it. She didn't need anyone telling her how to do things.

"Mark, I don't…"

"If you don't I'll have to turn you in. Neither of us wants that. I know John wouldn't want that and it would cause problems for me at home as well. You're just too likeable of a person and you've become a pain in my ass because of it."

Miranda laughed a little. She hadn't thought about it quite like that. He had a point, though. She was crazy about John and didn't want to risk losing him. She also had to admit that Mark's family had made an incredible impression on her as well. They made her want to settle down and start a family of her own, but she felt torn with her own moral complexities to follow through. Maybe this would be the compromise she needed to transition into a normal life. She could step away and let someone else be the protector from time to time.

"Okay," she sighed, "I'll give it a try. How would this work?"

Mark smiled. His life just got less complicated and he had at least a minimal support team to work with now. Better yet, maybe he had someone he could actually *talk* to about jobs other than John. That would help a lot in dealing with the stresses of the work load.

"It's pretty simple," He started, "John gives me a dossier on a target. I work off the information I have available to figure out when and where the individual might be to take them down. A little field recon helps to get a feel for the location and possible vantage points to take the shot from. Target sticks his head out; I pull the trigger. The Chief moves some money around and I get paid."

"So, the Chief is the one who assigns the targets?"

"It's a collaboration of sorts. I'm not sure who is involved, but I know he and John are the ones who put the packets together for me.

"That's another thing; nobody knows who I am and now nobody can know who you are either. We work in secret and because of that, we are also on the wanted list."

"Even though we work for the police?"

"Even though we work for the police. The Chief doesn't need the legal complications of hiring a hit man, so he doesn't want to know anything about who I am or what I do. He just wants the bad elements of the city eliminated."

"So, he doesn't know who you are? I thought you worked at the department."

"I do, on a contract basis for simple repairs and such. He has no idea what I really do for him besides change light bulbs and fix doors. He doesn't want to know either and I'll gladly not say a word about it."

Miranda studied the situation for a moment. Simple. Yeah, right.

"So, let me see if I'm following this correctly. Chief Dahlgren and John collect information on criminals and put them into a file for you.

You take the file and plan out how to kill the bad guy. Then, when you've taken the guy out, the Chief shuffles the books to pay you for the job."

"Right."

"The Chief doesn't know who you are, even though you see him all the time and work at the department a lot. And because you are killing people you are wanted by the police, even though you are working under the direction of the CLEO."

"You got it. See? Simple."

"Essentially, every cop in town is out to arrest you except for Dahlgren and my boyfriend."

"Right. That's why it is critical to leave no traces behind. No footprints, no casings, no fingerprints, no anything. Just a body. You've already figured that out and do a pretty good job of it. As a matter of fact, John asked me if *I* was the one going around popping these guys that *you* have been taking out. The scenes were very sanitary."

Miranda smiled shyly.

"Sorry about that. I didn't know it was you I was copying. I just knew that someone had been picking bad guys off for a while and the cops never found any evidence. Sounded like the right way to do it to me.

"Okay, I have a question. Well, actually, I have a LOT of questions, but this one springs to mind first. I only have my Glock. All the work you do seems to be long range. Are you wanting me to do the close up stuff and you hang back?"

"No. I am not comfortable with getting in close. Distance is your friend, especially when you have multiple targets or, as John puts it, a 'target rich environment' to work in. I'm also uncomfortable with you being in the middle of a messy situation. Since I'm asking you for help, I want you to be as safe as I can get you on a job. That means distance. You used to shoot rifles on the ranch, right?"

"Yeah, but I haven't touched one in years. I'll need some practice."

"That's not a problem. I can help you there. If I can teach John how to run a rifle at long ranges against moving targets, I can teach you."

Miranda laughed, "Was he hard to teach?"

"A lot of guys are pre-wired to be the 'be all, end all' macho type, even if they don't show it. When you give a guy a gun, there isn't supposed to be any instruction necessary. We just know how it works. That makes us hard to teach because you have to untrain the ego before you can train the skills. Women don't have that problem as badly. That's why my daughter can practically outshoot me with a rifle and she's only thirteen."

"Okay, but I still don't have a rifle to learn with."

"Again, not a problem. I just happened to acquire one recently in a bit of a humanitarian effort that seems to be working out pretty well. I'll check it over and make sure it's in good order before you run it. Which reminds me, I've seen you pull two different jobs; one this morning and another a few weeks ago near a parking garage on 17th. I saw what you were wearing both times and I have to ask; where do you hide your pistol?"

Miranda smiled, almost blushing a little. She looked back at the entrance to the shop and said, "Come with me."

She stood and headed to the back of the shop. Mark followed, unsure of what he was about to learn or if he really wanted to know.

She led him into the small stock room at the back of the building and turned her back to the sales floor in case anyone walked in. Reaching up under her shirt Mark could hear the distinct sound of metal against plastic as she produced the weapon.

"It's called a Flashbang holster. You can't use it with too big of a frame, but for my little Model 43 it works really well."

She lifted the shirt tail up, exposing the tiny Kydex holster firmly attached to the webbing between the cups of her bra. Miranda snapped the pistol back in place and pulled the shirt tail back down. Mark was surprised at how well the whole system concealed.

"Wow," Mark said, "I'm impressed." He suddenly became aware that his eyes were still on her chest, "With the holster, I mean. That's pretty neat. The holster is. Neat, I mean."

Miranda just giggled. She hadn't seen Mark

flush red with embarrassment before. To think that he did the work he did and was that easily stammered was funny indeed.

"So," Miranda said, "Are you going to tell John?"

Mark was already walking back to the chairs at the front of the shop.

"That you showed me your boobs? Nope. Never going to say a word to anyone about that. I'd just as soon it was never brought up again."

Miranda laughed out loud, "No, I mean about what we talked about; about what I've been doing and everything."

Her smile began to fade as Mark turned to face her.

"Nope," his single word was absolute, "You will."

Chapter 22

Saturday morning found Mark on the rifle range once again. He placed targets on the field at various distances out to 250 yards and arranged the table and spotting scope for the day. Beside the spotting scope he positioned the AR-15 he had confiscated from Robinson. While not a top of the line model, it was a very good quality rifle with solid internals and an 18 inch barrel. He had a pair of magazines and a few boxes of ammunition beside it for when the sighting in session was complete.

In the case nearby was his M1A that he had purchased a few years earlier. It had proven quite handy on a few jobs where he needed quick follow up shots over a longer distance. While not quite the tack driver of his bolt action rifles, it was faster and accurate enough with a larger magazine capacity. He had replaced the original walnut stock with a Juggernaut Tactical Rogue model that significantly reduced the length and changed the center of balance to make a much faster handling and easier to conceal platform.

On the corner of the table he sat his range bag with the spare magazines and ammunition for his 1911 and a few first aid items, including a chemical ice pack for his ankle, along with spare eye and ear protection.

"It's better to have it and not need it than to need it and not have it," Himes' father used to say.

About 8:00 a silver Honda Accord approached the facility and soon Mark's pupil had arrived on the firing line.

"Good Morning!" Miranda said with a smile.

"Hey! Are you ready for this?"

She stepped under the shelter and deposited a bag on the opposite corner of the table from Mark's gear.

"I might as well be. I'm committed at this point," she rummaged through the reusable shopping bag producing a pair of hot coffees and two of the largest muffins Mark had ever seen.

"Well," He smiled, "I don't suppose we have to start right away, now do we?"

"My thoughts exactly," Miranda said as she hefted the styrene cup in a toast.

The pair sat at the bench and Mark began to explain the plan for the day. They would begin with some basic safety and operational points and then move into grip and trigger manipulation, then dry fire a few rounds to familiarize Miranda with the action and operation of the firearms. When she was comfortable enough they would move on to live fire and sight the rifle in.

She would begin with the AR-15 since Mark had planned on giving it to her anyway. He had no need for another rifle like that and if she was going to do this, she needed something.

Later he planned on introducing her to the M1A. Since she had used larger caliber bolt actions before, he wasn't too concerned about her being able to handle the power of the .308 caliber rifle, but he didn't want her to jump in with both feet on it either. Baby steps were best, even if the baby was learning to walk for a second time.

They finished their muffins and coffee and turned their attention to the weapons before them.

"Okay," Mark began, "This is the rifle I'm going to let you have. The young man this belonged to has since found Jesus and no longer needs the weapon, so it is in need of a new home. I don't need it at my house, so you are the new foster mother to this fine piece of hardware."

"Okay," Miranda replied, looking it over curiously.

"Do you know what it is?"

"It's an AR-15, isn't it?"

"Yes, it is. Have you ever shot one before?"

"No, I've never even picked one up before."

"Well, let's start with the rules first and then we'll cover the basics of the design."

"Rules?"

"Oh, yeah. Everybody has to know the rules of basic firearms safety or I'm not going to teach them anything. If you can't be safe with one, you certainly don't need to be dangerous with one."

Miranda smiled, "Alright, let's hear them."

"First: Always treat every firearm like it is loaded; even if it isn't.

"Second: Always be sure of your target and what is beyond it. A .22 long rifle bullet can travel a mile and a half. You can imagine what a larger caliber can do and you, as the shooter, are responsible for where it goes and where it stops.

"Third: Never point the firearm at anything you are not absolutely willing to destroy. That is particularly true for you and me.

"Fourth, and finally: Keep your finger off the trigger until you are ready to shoot. I don't care how many safeties you have on a firearm or whether they are internal or external or both; that finger and your brain are the ultimate safety features of any weapon. Use them, and know when not to use them."

Miranda nodded in agreement. She had heard her father go over these same rules with her when she lived at home and they would target shoot.

"Will there be a test?" she asked with a smile.

"Every time you pull a firearm out of storage, it's a test. When we go to do a job, it's more like a final exam. The pressure is on and you have to know what you're doing and keep your head about *why* you're doing it."

Mark looked at Miranda, studying her face carefully. He hated to sound like John, but felt it was necessary given the nature of their new relationship.

"Seriously, if you ever have problems dealing with this, let me or someone know. Your boyfriend is constantly on me about PTSD and mental stress because of these jobs. You have to handle them or they *will* handle you."

Miranda's smile faded a little as she nodded an understanding nod.

"Do you have any suggestions for how you deal with it? I mean, you don't seem like you're about to snap or anything."

Mark half smiled. He and John had embarked on this same conversation several times before, especially when the job was complicated.

"Some people are wired differently than others. Some folks can't open a jar of pickles without breaking down emotionally. Others could have a freight train run across their foot and never wince at the pain. Most of us are somewhere in the middle.

"Law enforcement can only do so much, and the Chief and John asked me to step in to a complicated situation to help out.

"I'm no good to them or my family if I can't handle the stress that comes with the work. I choose to deal with it the only way I know how. I have to prioritize the outcome as being for the greater good of my family, and by extension, my community. Mostly, I just don't think about it when I'm not on a job."

She sat silently, digesting the advice.

"Incidentally," Mark began, "How have you been dealing with it? To my understanding, you've been a busy girl this year."

"Work," she said, "I stay busy and it keeps

my mind occupied. I try not to dwell on the actual events, but they are always there."

She formulated her comments before continuing.

"I used to have nightmares. You know, after the first couple. I would wake up from a dream thinking that I had failed and was attacked myself or that someone I cared about was the victim because I couldn't be there to protect them. I haven't had those in a while."

"Ever throw up?"

"Yeah. A couple of times. A few hours later."

"Me too. I had to shoot a good friend of mine during a big take down. 'Target rich environment,' you might say."

Miranda just stared at Mark. She couldn't believe that he would shoot a friend to finish a job. Maybe she misunderstood.

"Did…did you just say you shot a friend on a job?"

"Yep."

Her face deeply reflected the astonishment

in her mind.

"Why did you do that? Did you kill him?"

Mark smiled, "He was on the wrong side of things and I needed him to change his perspective. I called him first to try and talk him out of what he was doing, but he rejected the offer. So, I put a bullet in his shoulder from about 800 yards away. I didn't know if I had killed him or not until long after the gunfight was over. That shot was pure luck. I puked my guts up on the way home. It was the most miserable I have ever felt in my life."

"Would you do it again?"

Mark thought hard about the answer.

"Yes. I would. That lucky shot got him out of the drug game and back into legal work. He's alive today because of a hard learned lesson that could have been his last. The fact that he cleaned himself up and turned his life back around is the final result. That's what I have to measure it by. I can't dwell on the fact that if the wind had changed direction I could have killed a good friend.

"Besides, he gave us a ton of information

that led to the arrest and elimination of a few big players in the crime industry around here. The community benefitted from his injuries as well."

Miranda was stunned. She had often heard of people making the hard choices in situations, but she had never actually met anyone that had to make a choice like that. She hoped that she was never in that situation herself.

"Okay," Mark said suddenly, "Time to get to work!"

He suddenly stood and motioned to the AR-15. Picking up the rifle, he began to point out the features of the design. Safety, magazine release, bolt release, charging handle, and all the other points and protrusions on the little aluminum receiver assemblies were quickly covered before he handed the weapon to her.

She sat in her seat, admiring the rifle and inspecting the components he had covered. She threw it up to her shoulder, keeping the muzzle pointed downrange, and looked across the iron sights. It was surprisingly light for the length and the adjustable stock would collapse to fit her length of pull needs very well.

They were soon running a dry firing session with an empty magazine to get her familiar with the trigger pull and charging handle operation. It wasn't long before they moved on to live fire.

Mark showed her how to sight in at 25 yards and then they dialed it on out to 100. He explained how the bullet would actually climb and fall after leaving the muzzle, so proper understanding of bullet flight was always a good idea when shooting longer distances.

Since the AR didn't have an optic for long range shots, they kept it to targets within 100 yards. Mark told Miranda that he thought he had a spare scope back at home that would work for the rifle if she was interested.

"You seem to be pretty comfortable with the platform," Mark said, "How would you feel about stepping up to a little larger caliber?"

"How much larger?" Miranda asked.

".308."

A smile broke across her face as she

flipped the safety on the AR, dropped the magazine and cleared the chamber.

"Bolt action?"

"Nope," Mark said as he reached for the case.

He placed the padded case on the table and opened it to reveal the scoped M1A inside. The stock showed some signs of wear, but the finish on the rifle was still in very good shape. Under the front handguard was a collapsible Harris bipod.

Miranda stared for a minute, then looked at Mark with an expression of disappointment.

"I was looking forward to something more familiar," she said.

"Well, we will work on that later. I wanted you to learn this one early on because I may have a use for it, and you, pretty soon."

Miranda's attention was suddenly diverted from weapon training.

"You have a contract?"

"I've had a contract. I now have multiple contracts. That's why I need your help."

She sat back down at the table.

"Well, don't keep me in suspense."

"A few weeks ago, John asked me if I could take out a local thug with cartel ties. It seems that he has been negotiating a connection to bring in more drugs, guns, and crime to our fair city. In return he hopes the cartel will give him the leverage he needs to take over control of a larger part of town. Since then, the contacts with the cartel have decided to drop by and see things first hand. That's where you come in."

"I'm listening."

"I have made multiple trips into town where the local guys call home. They have a formidable setup, using an old movie theater and some surrounding buildings for a headquarters kind of arrangement. They are running patrols in the surrounding neighborhoods and even have aerial surveillance with a drone now. It's a messy spot, but I only need to take one guy out there. Then I need to figure out how to get out of there before all hell breaks loose and they find out where I am.

"On the other end of the spectrum are the visitors. They are flying in on the morning of the 24th at McClendon Field. Lots of open area and unobstructed fields of fire. No houses or roads nearby, so the shots would be cleaner. Therein lies the problem. There are going to be a minimum of five targets on the ground there. Probably more. Another thing is that if they get close to the buildings they can use the hangars and other aircraft for cover, possibly getting away.

"I can't be in both places at once, but if I try to get all the targets at once, at either location, I'll be outgunned and stand a better chance of getting myself caught."

"Or killed," Miranda added.

"Yeah, or killed," Mark agreed, "So, I need an extra set of eyes to look this mess over and help me pull this off. What do you say?"

Miranda slumped back in the chair and ran her hand across her forehead.

"Where do you need me to be?"

"Let's finish range time up and take a drive. In the meantime, are you ready to run this?"

Mark gestured again to the M1A.

"Show me how it works."

After they packed up for the day Mark and Miranda made a special trip to the airport to see the second objective first hand.

The area was relatively flat with only some very gentle slopes on the western side. The hangars and terminal were situated somewhat in the middle with some newer hangars just north of them, on the other side of the fuel tanks.

A twin pair of 10,000 gallon tanks of aviation fuel sat in the midst of it all, with a handful of private aircraft scattered about the tarmac. For the most part the airport was typically deserted except for a minimal staff of administrative people and mechanics. On weekends and at night there wasn't a soul to be found.

To both the east and west of the runways, and behind the hangars, were thick woods. Draped across the low lying hills the thickets and scrub brush concealed the roots of countless fir and deciduous trees that helped to serve as a wind break and a noise buffer to the outside world.

The pair pulled in at the terminal and approached the door. Mark's mind was racing to come up with something to say in case they were questioned about their presence.

"Good afternoon," a voice called from the counter at the opposite side of the building, "How can I help you?"

Leaning across the counter slightly was a short fellow with thinning white hair, silver framed glasses and a white beard trimmed and neat.

Before Mark could say a word Miranda was already talking.

"Hi! We were wondering if you could give us some information about flights and schedules. We've been thinking about taking a little vacation soon and, well, we just don't care much for the idea of the big commercial flights. All that waiting and crowds and everything."

"Absolutely. Where were you thinking of going?"

Miranda shot Mark a glance and she was met with a blank face, so she carried on.

"We have been talking about going somewhere fun. Maybe down to the Florida Keys or even out to New Mexico."

"Well, let's just cover the basics then, shall we?"

The gentleman proceeded to outline how the pricing broke down for a flight, the cost of fuel and the storage of the plane and per diem for the pilot while on the trip. The other option was to pay for a flight down and an empty flight of the pilot and plane back, then the opposite when you were ready to return. Either way it was rather pricey.

"You can see why most folks don't do long trips with chartered aircraft. If you can split your costs with some other folks it makes it a bit easier to handle."

"Yes," Miranda said, "I can see how it would be rather expensive. Still, there is the convenience of not having to deal with big city traffic and lines, and all that.

"You mentioned splitting the cost with others. How many people can you fit on a plane at an airport this size?"

The man pointed out the window to a twin engine Beechcraft just outside.

"We can haul six passengers and two flight crew in that one. Sometimes we get bigger planes in here, though. Since we have one of the longest runways in the region, we've had small jets and even some bigger turbo props drop in for fuel and maintenance over the years.

"I guess the biggest one we've ever had here was probably that C-130 that dropped in back in the 1980's. They had some mechanical issues and needed to do some repairs. That's a pretty good sized aircraft."

"Does anyone here fly a jet? That might be a fun vacation, with a private jet and all."

"No ma'am. None of us can afford one. There are some that come in from time to time, though."

"Is there any way to know when one might be coming in, so we could see how much it would cost to charter a jet?"

"No, unfortunately. For the most part domestic flights within the U.S. aren't required to file flight plans and even when they are you have a small window to file. You can even file them after you take off, so we never know who's coming or when unless they call ahead."

"Oh," Miranda said with a little frustration in her tone, "Well, that's alright. We'll just take a look online and see what we can find. Thank you for your time."

"My pleasure, ma'am. If you decide to charter a flight through any of our local pilots, just call the office and we'll be glad to take you where you want to go. Sorry I couldn't be more help."

Mark and Miranda headed out the front door and back to her car. Once they were on the road Mark sighed and looked out the window.

"What's wrong?"

"I was hoping for a lot more information, that's all."

"Well, we at least know that they won't be expecting them. We also know about what size plane it will be and we know how the place is laid out. That's more than we had when we came out."

"I guess. Well, it's time to start detailing this plan. Time is running out."

Over the next several days Mark and Miranda spent time almost daily at the range brushing up on her long range skills. The one disappointing issue that always came up was that there was no ideal way to train for moving targets at distance.

Though she had become rather proficient with the M1A and the AR-15 in those sessions, Mark worried that the target environment might be more than she was able to handle. He had been there before and it could get very tricky.

Chapter 23

Mark's phone rang early that morning. He was already on the way into town, but the sudden ringing caught him off guard.

"Hello?"

"Hey, man," John said in an almost cheerful tone, "What's going on?"

"Making a quick trip into town. You?"

"Nothing much. I have some paperwork for you to look over if you have a few minutes."

"Alright. Can you meet me somewhere?"

"Sure give me a time and place."

Mark thought carefully about his plans for the day and finally spoke up.

"I'll tell you what, just meet me at Miranda's store in about thirty minutes. Will that work?"

"I get to drop this crap off to you *and* get to see my girl? Yeah, that will work."

Mark could hear the smile on John's face

through the phone.

"Good deal," he said, "I'll see you there."

A little while later John arrived at the shop and parked out front. Mark's truck was already there and he could see his friend sitting in a chair at the front of the building with a cup of coffee and a massive croissant on a plate in front of him.

John strode in the front door and headed for the chairs. Miranda stepped out of the back room and waved as he made his way across the room.

As he maneuvered to sit he handed a large manila envelope to Mark.

"That's for you. Some information on that company you've been looking into and also payment for that 'repair' job you did."

Mark opened the envelope and saw a tidy stack of bills nestled among several sheets of paper with photographs printed on them.

Miranda stepped up and grabbed John around the neck as Mark closed the envelope and laid it on the table.

"Hi, honey," she said as she squeezed him

tightly and planted a kiss on his cheek, "What brings you here?"

John gestured across the table to Mark, "This guy. Trying to pay him for some work he did and I have to track him all over town. He's always on the go. I should have known I'd find him where the coffee is fresh, the food is free and the view is fantastic," he looked Miranda up and down as he uttered his last word, bringing a slight blush to her cheeks.

"Hey," Mark snapped, "I'll have you know I pay for all my food here. I'm not a freeloader, you know."

"That's right," Miranda interjected, "He does pay for all the food. Not the coffee, mind you, but the food, he does," she smiled at Mark with a twinkle in her eyes.

John turned his attention back to Mark.

"So, there's an itemized list of things for the next job the Chief wants you to work on in there. Do you need me to cover that with you or are you good?"

Mark kicked back in the chair, as calm and

collected as a professional poker player.

"Nah. If I have any questions, I know where you live. I'll look it over in a while and get started on it."

"I kind of figured you would," John replied. He looked at his watch and began to stand, "Well, fun time is over. I have to get back to the mines."

Miranda pouted her lip as he turned to face her. John met the pout with a kiss and a smile and then looked back at Mark.

"Nope, I don't need a kiss. Besides, I'm married," Mark joked, his finger pointing to the ring on his left hand.

John chuckled and headed for the door with Miranda in tow.

"I'll call you later, Okay?" He said as he reached for the knob.

"You'd better," She said with a smile.

A final kiss and the two parted ways. After a few minutes Miranda approached Mark and sat down in John's former seat.

Mark looked around the shop as if he were

about to unveil the secrets of life for only her to hear.

"Do you have a little more private area I could use for a minute?"

"Sure," she said as she stood, "you can use the stockroom. There's also a small bathroom back there if you need it."

The pair headed for the back of the building where Mark stepped aside of the doorway and produced the stack of cash from the envelope.

Quickly counting it up, he then divided it into two equal shares and handed Miranda one.

"What's this for?'

"Your half for the job in the park."

Miranda was surprised enough that she stammered for words momentarily before blurting, "But, I didn't have the contract. You did."

"Yeah," Mark responded, "But you were just as involved in the take down as I was. Maybe more, I don't know. I figure you earned half anyway. I've never had to split a payment before. Is that fair enough for you?"

Miranda stood there staring back and forth

between Mark's face and the bills in her hand.

"Yeah, I guess so. I never really thought about getting paid to do the job is all."

"Well, if you don't want the money," Mark smiled, "I have kids to put through college in a few years…"

"No," She replied quickly, "We're good here. I'll stuff this away in my cookie jar at home."

Her gaze shifted back to the envelope.

"So, what else is in there?"

Mark peeled open the flap again, "Looks like our guests have faces after all."

He looked around the room for a table or anything to use as a substitute.

"I wish I was at my shop," he finally said, "I could lay all this out on my work bench and see what we have coming our way."

"Come on," Miranda said, "We can use the room upstairs. I have a table up there."

She led him to the corner where a narrow set of wooden steps led up over the bathroom into the upper floor space. It was a single large room with hardwood floors and exposed brick walls.

Boxes of miscellaneous items were stacked here and there. Along the wall to the right sat a large table with a lamp on it and a couple of folding chairs rested against the wall beside it.

"I thought about using this room for my contract IT work, but I just never got around to it."

Mark dumped the contents of the envelope onto the table top and began to sort through the data.

He lined up the mug shots and then each corresponding page of information for each suspect was stacked beneath them.

"Santiago Rodriguez," Mark said, "Looks like he is the Colombian connection. Drug charges on him, mostly. I'd say he is the pharmaceutical man."

He leaned over and scanned the next pages as Miranda read them aloud.

"Misha Kedzierski.. This is my kind of guy. Human trafficking and potential terrorist ties. Ukranian."

"Roberto Dominguez is the socialite of the

group. Multiple counts of kidnapping and extortion. He also has a healthy list of suspected cartel connections and drug charges. I'll bet he's the life of the party," Mark muttered.

"Oh, a family connection," Miranda continued, "Dokka Shishani and Bekhan Maskadov are cousins from Chechnya."

Mark leaned over to see their sheets as Miranda scanned their histories.

"Wow," he said as she read it off.

"Weapons smuggling, suspected connections to multiple terrorist events across Europe, bomb making, and more human trafficking. These guys are the real deal," she laid the pages down and scanned the entire table trying to digest it all.

Mark pulled over one of the folding chairs and sat down, also studying the international assembly.

"This was not what I was expecting," Miranda finally said.

The chime rang on her front door, indicating a customer's arrival downstairs.

"Excuse me," was all she said as she

quickly headed for the steps.

Mark began to shuffle through the paperwork for each individual and noticed that John had scribbled a price on each one. Apparently, there was a substantial amount of money already available for their capture or termination. Mark would have to follow up on how that would work since he would be eliminating them covertly and couldn't risk having his cover blown. He certainly didn't want Miranda exposed either.

His biggest fear, though, was that if their identities were revealed it might bring international elements down on them. The last thing he needed in his life was a blood thirsty international criminal organization out for revenge.

Still, when all the rewards were tallied it came to a considerable amount of money. Mark also knew that in many cases if the individuals were killed or captured by law enforcement the rewards were usually not paid. There was no way the Chief could move this much money around in the budget without someone noticing. Himes wondered if the budget was even as big as the reward money.

After several minutes Miranda reappeared at the top of the steps.

"So," she began, "what's the plan?"

"Pull up a chair. I have an idea."

Miranda unfolded the other chair and slid it up beside Mark.

"Okay," Mark said fumbling for a pen or pencil that seemed to elude him, "You've seen the airport. I'm thinking we use the tree lines to cover these guys. When the plane lands, they will all have to get out. That's the best opportunity to catch them. The doorway will be like a 'fatal funnel' that they all will have to go through. We will need to make sure that the plane can't take off also.

"So, when it lands, the first shot needs to take out a tire or something. Something needs to happen to disable the plane. I don't want them to have the opportunity to leave."

Miranda nodded her head in agreement as Mark continued.

"At this point I don't have any reason to believe that any of the flight crew are anything but that; a flight crew. I could be wrong, but based on what we know these are the only targets we have on that plane.

"These guys need to be eliminated as soon as the last one is in the door. If you drop him in the doorway, the others won't be able to get back onboard quickly. If the plane is down, they can't leave anyway. Then it becomes a matter of picking the others off before they get to cover. That means we'll have to use something accurate and powerful, which is why we've been running the M1A lately. Being a semi-automatic will get us faster follow up shots and being a .308…"

"Will get us the stopping power we'll need to drop them at distance," Miranda concluded, "What about them getting to cover? What if they leave the plane and immediately make for some kind of building or something?"

Mark thought about it for a minute. They could stay on the aircraft until their escorts arrived and then go from one vehicle to another and not present an opportunity. Then again, if that were a major concern, they probably wouldn't be flying into a small regional airport.

"I'm banking on the notion that they are using McClendon Field because they are trying to avoid security risks. A smaller field outside of town is less likely to be monitored by anyone and should allow them to let their guard down a little. Not a lot, mind you, but hopefully enough."

"What about the staff? Do we tell them what's about to happen?"

"No. We can't risk it. I wish we could, but I don't see how we can tell them to evacuate without exposing ourselves. Besides, if we tell them what's going to happen, they'll be calling the police before we can get the job done."

"Yeah, well, they'll be calling the police anyway once bullets start flying around those fuel tanks," Miranda added.

"Yes, but that's OK. By the time the police get there we should be done and on our way out. They can clean up the mess and do their investigation. With any luck they'll think the gang members and the cartel guys had a disagreement and it went off the rails from there."

"Speaking of the way out…" Miranda let the thought hang like a carrot before a horse.

"Oh, yeah. In and out. I've been thinking about that too," Mark said, "Man, I wish I had some paper and a pen or a map or something."

"Hang on, I'll be back in a second," Miranda headed for the stairs once again.

She had barely reached the floor below when Mark heard the front door chimes again. After several more minutes Miranda finally reappeared with a tablet computer and an ink pen in her hands.

She quickly brought the tablet online and pulled up an aerial view of the airport and surrounding properties.

"That's perfect," Mark smiled, "Now, look here." He indicated with the capped end of the ballpoint pen a tree line that extended almost due west of the airport to a small tertiary road. The tree line also connected to the thick wooded area along the western edge of the airport property.

"I'm thinking we use the cover of this old fence row here to slip into the trees overlooking the airport. We can come in early in the morning and hike in. We set up in this area and that will give us the concealment we need to take the shots from. When the job is done, we go back out the way we came in. Easy, peasey."

Miranda shot him a look of concern.

"Easy peasey? Really?"

"What?"

"How far of a hike in is that?'

"I don't know. It shouldn't be too far. Maybe a few hundred yards?"

Miranda slid her finger across the screen, selecting a measuring tool from the menu bar at the top and proceeded to measure the straight line distance along the fence row.

"That's nearly 1400 feet," she said flatly.

"So, roughly a quarter mile. No problem. I've done that in town lots of times."

"So have I, but not while carrying a rifle and ammunition with my adrenaline pumping through the roof."

Mark smiled, "Yeah, you get used to it."

She suddenly realized who she was talking

to and backed off the argument. After a few minutes of thought she asked, "So, are we both going in then?"

Mark sighed and leaned back in his chair.

"I'm not sure on that point," he said, "I'd like to take out the escorts before they get there. The original target is going to be with them. That will keep the opposition at the airfield to a minimum. The downside is that there are multiple targets at the airfield.

"Basically it boils down to a gut decision. Do we let them all get on site at the airport and then have a bigger firefight with the staff in the mix or do we split them up and take out the escorts at the theater while the other person takes out the cartel at the airport?"

Miranda and Mark both thought about the options in silence for a few minutes.

"You've been to the theater, right?"

"Several times," Mark replied.

"So, you're more familiar with what to expect there than I am. I feel confident that either of us could do the airport job."

"Agreed."

"Since that's the case, the only logical answer I can come up with is that you hit the theater and I take the airport. We take them out as smaller targets and minimize the exposure of the airport staff to a gunfight.

"The police will be called to both locations and, like you said, they can clean up while we slip away. What do you think? Will that work?"

Mark scratched his chin subconsciously as he mulled her idea over. It made sense. He wasn't entirely comfortable sending her out alone to face down the people coming in, but he was less comfortable with the idea of her being at the theater.

"Are you sure about that?"

"Yeah," she finally said, "yeah, I'm good. Do you think anyone will bother my car on the back road there?"

"No, because it won't be there," Mark answered, "I'll drop you in before sunrise and you hike in. When it's done, I'll swing back through and pick you up. No traces can be left behind, you know what I mean. If anyone saw your car on the road it might lead to questions and if they run your tags…"

"Good point. So, how will we stay in touch? I'll have to be able to contact you to keep you updated."

Mark reached in his pocket and produced his burn phone.

"Call me on this number," he said, "I wish I had a burn phone for you, but I don't just keep them lying around. Text might be better. Just keep the message vague enough that it won't draw attention."

"You mean I can't send you a text saying, 'Come get me. I just killed five members of an international crime cartel and I need you to pick me up on Anderson Road west of the airport'?" She giggled.

Mark laughed, "That might be a little obvious."

"Alright, I'll think of something. I may pick up a phone this afternoon to keep things cleaner too."

"That would be a good idea."

Chapter 24

Mark swung by Miranda's apartment early on Friday morning. She opened the door to his pickup truck and plopped in the passenger seat wearing a brown wig and ball cap.

"Say, do I know you?" Mark played, "I think I've seen you before."

"Well, I don't know. Do you ever go to Carson Park?"

Mark smiled back at her.

"What's with the hair?" he finally asked.

"I thought it might blend in better than my usual rosy locks. And I really didn't think the blonde one would work at all. It's supposed to be pretty sunny today, you know."

She glanced at the pair of duffel bags between them curiously. Before she could ask Mark answered.

"One is yours and the other is mine. Yours has the M1A and a couple of spare magazines along with a small first aid kit, just in case. There are also a couple of bottles of water and some granola bars in case you want breakfast or brunch, or whatever."

"Aw," she said sarcastically, "Always thinking of others. That's so sweet."

"Yeah, well, the 'others' I'm mostly thinking about are the ones on the plane. I also put a suppressor in there. Be sure to use it to keep your location as secret as possible. Do you remember how to put it on?"

"Yes. I remember. I was going to ask about that, but I didn't get to it yet. I'm thinking I should disable the plane while the engines are still running to use the noise to my advantage."

"That's a good idea. Are you ready for this?"

Miranda took a deep breath and announced, "Well, if I'm not I guess we'll find out around 8:00."

She successfully managed to talk him into grabbing a couple of biscuits at one of the local fast food drive through windows before heading out of town. Mark didn't much care for the food at places like that, but he had to admit he was glad to have something on his stomach, even if it was fast food.

After a while they arrived on Anderson Road and Mark slowed to a stop near the fence row from the aerial photo.

"Here's your stop, lady."

Miranda looked out across the darkened fields and tree line before grabbing her bag.

"I'll contact you when I'm in position," she said as she hefted the bag onto her shoulder.

"Be careful. I don't want to have to explain anything to anyone, OK?" Mark said as he watched her gear up.

Miranda smiled a nervous smile and closed the truck door. Within a few seconds she was over the fence and heading down the tree line toward the airport.

Mark pulled away and began his move to the theater.

About 4:15 in the morning Mark got a text from Miranda. She had reached her vantage point and was setting up her hide site. Mark, meanwhile, was in the parking garage and heading down to street level. Soon he'd be in the outer fringe of the neighborhood and moving in to the school. He was a bit nervous about using the building again, but it provided him with the best angle for the shot. It also provided him with the worst options to get out.

Because of the concerns he had, Mark had outfitted himself with a special tool for the job: a collapsible grappling hook and rope. He remembered a rooftop access hole in one of the upper floor rooms, but it didn't have a ladder or stairway to it. If he could use it to reach the roof, he could stay out of the way of the patrols. Then he'd only have to figure out how to get out.

To help with that he also packed a small bore camera that he had used for cleaning and inspecting his rifle barrels. It plugged into the accessory port on his phone and gave a reasonably clear image. He hoped it would come in handy for getting down off the roof when the time came.

Using his night vision monocular again, he

quickly made his way through the back alleys and side streets until he was within sight of the building. He waited in the shadow of some thick hedges and studied the structure for several minutes before moving in closer.

Just as he approached the building, he could hear voices around the corner. A patrol was on the grounds and moving his direction. He slipped silently to a small collection of trash barrels in a dark corner and squatted down, hoping they were careless enough not to inspect them closely.

A flashlight beam quickly panned the area, but continued on as the patrol members never skipped a beat in their conversation. Himes was getting closer to his objective, but he wasn't in yet. Next was actually getting inside the building undetected. He would relax a tiny bit once he was on the roof and secure.

He stepped through an old door that was slightly ajar, inspecting it with the monocular before committing himself fully. A short set of steps to his left led down to lower floor classrooms while the steps to the right would bring him to a pair of landings at the second and third floors. He scanned the entry carefully and listened for any indication of life inside the building before moving upward.

As he reached the halfway point on the stairwell, moving slowly and cautiously, he felt a tug at his pant leg. Immediately Himes stopped and peered down with the monocular. He could see his pant leg was distorted, as if a string was across it, but he couldn't see the string in the darkness. Running the risk of being seen, he slipped the monocular into his pocket for a minute and quickly shined his small pocket sized flashlight down to his feet. There, stretched across the steps, was a thin strand of monofilament.

"*Trip wires?*" Mark thought to himself. If there were trip wires, there had to be something to trip. What had they used? An alarm of some sort or some kind of anti-personnel device? Himes recalled John telling him that some of these guys had military experience and he remembered that in an earlier job he had done they confiscated some military grade explosives.

Mark smiled to himself as he put the flashlight away for a minute, "*Rat Face*," he thought. That was the armorer who had been modifying weapons and equipping local criminals for an income. He was the one that had stockpiled the explosives as well. Perhaps these people were some of his clientele.

Through the monocular Mark scanned the stairwell. There, under the treads of the next flight of steps he saw a curious looking box. On the side was a small pin that looked like a safety pin from a grenade or something. He couldn't tell what it was or what it could do, but decided to lightly step over the wire and proceed. If this way was wired, the others probably were as well. He would just have to remember to come down easy or find another way altogether.

Miranda made herself comfortable among the branches of some thick juniper brush and began to assemble the suppressor to the rifle. After a few turns of the device it was securely attached and ready for service. She extended the bipod legs and positioned the firearm in the direction of the tarmac ahead. The strobes and runway lights gave an almost surreal glow to the woods. All around her was silence with the exception of the tree frogs and crickets. Their constant droning and chirping was enough to ensure her alertness, but it also had a rhythm to it; melodic in a way.

She checked the time; 4:46 a.m. The sun would be up in a couple of hours and the plane should be along soon after that. To ease her nerves, she reached into the bag and pulled out a bottle of water. Though she was tempted to turn it up and swill it all down with a fervor, she decided that it might be wiser not to. She would hate to be caught out here with no bathroom in sight and bad guys on the ground. The thought of being "caught with your pants down" took on a new context in her mind and she smiled at the silliness of the thought.

About 5:10 a single car approached the main building. She couldn't tell who it was, but it didn't seem to be in a hurry, so she doubted it was any gang members out for a security check.

Soon the vehicle came to a stop across from the main building entrance and she could make out the silhouette of a figure getting out. As the individual approached the building she could tell it was the little man that she had spoken to with Mark. He was in the lighted entry of the building and was soon inside. After a couple of minutes some extra lights flickered on in one of the corners of the building. His day had started., and oh, what a day it would be.

Mark made his way through the upper floors without any further booby trap encounters and soon found himself at the roof access hole. He removed the small bag containing the grappling hook and rope and listened again for any signs he wasn't alone before fixing the tines and tossing the device through the hole. He pulled the excess rope back down until the claws of the hook grabbed firmly onto the frame of the hole. A couple of firm tugs let him know it was sturdy enough to climb, so he tied his duffel bag to the rope and began to climb up. His ankle was considerably better, but it still hurt quite a bit from time to time. Hopefully he wouldn't aggravate it too much getting out of here. Once he was on top, he pulled his bag up and left it attached to the rope.

Himes removed the rifle and magazines and a bottle of water, then slinked across the roof to overlook the theater. The sun would be up soon, and his target should be on the move soon after.

He quickly assembled the rifle and propped it up on the edge of the façade, pointing it toward the building in the distance.

Through his scope he could clearly see the rooftop positions and the people that manned them. He worried that they might spot him and considered taking them out first, but that might give him away before he could complete the contract. No, his first shot had to be to take down the leader. With any luck, it would be the only shot he'd need to take.

The thought made him reach into the inside pocket of his jacket. He produced a small block of steel with a spring loaded lever on one side; an odd looking device that John had given him after the raid on Rat Face's workshop. This particular drop in auto sear, or DIAS as they were called, never made it into the evidence room. Mark slipped back to the bag and removed his compact AR. He deftly broke it down, inserting the device behind the fire control group, then quietly closed the receivers back together and pushed the take down pin back into place.

Mark had never used the device on a job, but he had played with it a few times at home and it did exactly what it was supposed to: turn a semi-automatic rifle into a fully automatic one.

Manufacturing of these devices was prohibited with the 1986 machinegun ban, but apparently Rat Face had no problems with breaking the law. What used to be a $50 device in the early 1980's was now a felony to possess, unless it was a legally registered one, of course. Then it became a $50 device with a $20,000 price tag and a $200 piece of paper saying you could own it.

Himes quietly crawled back to the edge of the building and opened the water. On the street below he could hear another patrol on the move. He checked his watch. It was just after 5:20 a.m.

At 7:20 the airport came to life as the mechanics and pilots began to arrive. Miranda counted seven people that had come in so far that morning and most were in the main hangar. A couple had moved to the smaller private hangars out back and the little man was still in the main building. Before long a small tug towed a single engine Cessna 180 out into the sunshine. She peered through the scope and could see a second aircraft being prepared for flight as well.

Soon after, the Cessna growled to life and began to taxi toward the runway. She panned back to the fuel tanks and could see the twin engine Beechcraft was beginning to fuel up. Manning the pump was the little man from earlier. She wondered if he would be the pilot.

At 7:48 the Beechcraft, under the command of the little white haired man, began to speed down the runway as well. Soon the airport was quiet again, with the exception of some classic rock and roll that seemed to emanate from within the main hangar.

Six minutes later Miranda could hear the distinctive whine of jet engines in the distance.

At 6:36 Mark noticed an increase of activity on the back side of the theater. Below him, inside the school, he clearly heard the radio chatter and conversations of a patrol searching the building. It was the first one he had heard inside the structure all morning. Hopefully it would be the last.

By 6:49 the building was again silent and he watched the patrol work their way to the south of his position.

Quickly he moved his equipment back to the roof access hole and began to pack things loosely into the bag. He pulled the bore camera out of his pants pocket and attached it to the phone.

Himes slipped the camera over the opening and bent it down into the upper floor space, panning it around slowly as he watched the grainy image on his telephone screen. Through the dimness of the early morning light, he could see that there wasn't anyone on the upper floor, so he began to lower his gear back down, followed soon after by himself.

Mark made his way to a window just below where he had been on the roof and again set himself up a sniping position. As he panned the theater he noticed the familiar shape of the drone box beside the front sandbag emplacement. He hadn't seen it flying, but it was at least ready to use.

At 7:24 the roof top team picked up a couple of extra hands. A slim man with a baggy shirt arrived with a bolt action rifle in his hands and a cigarette in his mouth. Mark assumed it was the 'left handed' variety.

Eight minutes later the back door of the theater opened and four members of a security detail stepped out, flanking the doorway on either side. A pair of men exited the building and made their way to a pair of black sedans parked with their back bumpers toward the building. They quickly started the engines as one of the security team opened a door to the vehicle on the right.

At 7:36 Mark flipped the safety off on the rifle and began to press the trigger.

Chapter 25

The Gulfstream was a beautiful aircraft as it leveled off on final approach and touched down on the runway. Miranda thought how nice it must be to have one of the thirty million dollar aircraft. Perhaps one day she would know, but not today. Today she had to make sure it didn't fly out.

The plane approached from the northern end of the field and taxied back to the main building from the south end of the runway. The Rolls Royce turbines made quite a sound as the jet slowly bounced along the asphalt.

Miranda slipped her finger up to the safety on the trigger guard and pressed it to the left, unlocking the rifle's action. She had chambered a round when she inserted the magazine, so that step was already done. She calculated the distance the way Mark had told her and focused on the left rear landing gear. About 400 yards from the terminal, where the plane would still be fully exposed and no cover was available, she pressed the trigger.

The 168 grain projectile coughed from the muzzle and raced toward the aircraft, piercing the tire and sending shards of shredded rubber across the asphalt surface. Immediately the plane lurched to a stop as the pilot jammed on the brakes to prevent further damage to the landing gear.

The whine of the engines began to soften as the pilot, no doubt, tried to assess the situation. After a few minutes the side door opened and a man stepped into the doorway wearing a white shirt with insignia on the shoulders.

"That would be the pilot," Miranda thought, *"Come on and get out of my way."*

As the pilot cleared the stairs and spotted the damaged tire, another figure appeared in the doorway. Holding a glass in his left hand, the figure gestured frantically at the uniformed man who held up a reassuring hand in reply. Miranda wasn't positive, but she thought the second man was Maskadov.

Soon there was more movement at the doorway. The passengers didn't seem to be very worried about a security issue as the pilot was apparently blaming the condition of the rural airstrip for the loss of the tire.

One by one the passengers exited the plane to see for themselves the damage that the aircraft had suffered. First came Maskadov, then Shishani, then a dark haired Latino woman, followed by Dominguez and Rodriguez. Finally Kedziersky stepped into the doorway with a svelte blonde at his side. Her blouse flared open in the breeze as she snuggled up to him, trying to see what all the commotion was about.

Miranda exhaled slightly and pressed the trigger again.

Mark's primary target stepped through the back door of the building with a cell phone up to his ear. He nodded his head and checked his watch before ending the call and shoving the device in his pants pocket. As he was speaking to the security man on his right, the .308 ball slammed him in the chest, knocking him instantly to the ground. The team reacted almost immediately with the security man grabbing the leader and beginning to drag him to cover. Mark pressed the trigger again, dropping the security man on the asphalt.

He peered through the scope and saw the leader was still moving, trying desperately to pull himself to cover behind a vehicle. A third shot stopped him cold.

The wall around Mark's window suddenly burst into tiny fragments of masonry and the slim smoker on the roof zeroed in on his position. He'd been spotted and the patrols would now be on their way as well.

Himes moved to the next window and slipped the muzzle of his rifle out through the broken pane, quickly finding the sniper and pressing the trigger. The round was on, but unfortunately impacted the sandbags in front of the man's face. The smoker was hidden well behind the bags, giving Himes only a thin, small portion of the top of his head for a target, and much of it was obscured by the scope.

Himes slid back to the opposite side of the window and quickly got the man in his crosshairs again as the brick and block erupted inside the room. The shot was high, but probably would have been fatal had Mark not moved.

He fired again, spraying the man's optics with dust and debris from inside the bag. As the man shifted to clean the lens Mark ran the bolt and fired again. He saw a brief spray of crimson and the rifle fell unceremoniously to the roof top. Himes watched the position for a few seconds to be sure the man was down and then pulled back the magnification. The security teams had split up and were hiding behind the cars. The drivers were still in the vehicles and were waving frantically for the others to jump in so they could get away from the area.

Mark took two more shots, each piercing the radiators and fracturing the blocks on the automobiles. He decided it was time to break down and move before the school was saturated with bad guys.

The heat buildup in the barrel and receiver had served to tightly bond the two sections together, making it impossible for Mark to break them apart without a vise. He would have to carry the weapon fully assembled until it cooled down. He rammed the rifle into his bag and quickly pulled the compact AR out, slipping the suppressor on and shoving a fresh magazine of 300 Blackout into the well.

As he began to make his way toward the nearest set of steps he could hear voices below. Radios crackled as the teams tried to find his location. Then he heard a new sound: the buzz of electric motors outside the window. As he turned he saw the drone hovering just outside the glass. With his face mask up he wasn't worried about identification, but as long as that thing was flying he could be tracked.

"Time to swat the fly," Himes mumbled.

He spun around and brought the tiny rifle to bear, using the red dot sight to put a bead on the flying menace and pressed the trigger.

The lag time to transmit video back to the operator was enough to make sure the reaction was slow and the rifle round slammed into the frame of the drone. The aircraft tumbled as it shattered with chunks of plastic and electronics bleeding from it as it fell.

Mark began to rush toward the stairway he came in from. As he neared a mid-structure hallway he skidded to a stop. Around the corner, pistols drawn, stepped Adam Robinson.

Kedzierski's body dropped straight to the floor of the aircraft and flopped lifelessly onto the folding steps. The blond stood for a moment in total shock before screaming something inaudible and ducking back inside the aircraft.

With the engines still turning, the scream was scrambled among the turbine whine, but enough to get the attention of Shishani and Maskadov who looked back to see the torso twisted and draped across the steps.

Immediately the pair drew weapons from under their jackets and began to scan the area. Rodriguez and Dominguez noted their reaction and drew their own weapons as well and made their way cautiously back to the aircraft ramp. As they did so the small tug approached from the main hangar. The driver, seeing them pull their weapons, suddenly stopped the vehicle and turned about as quickly as he could, heading back to the safety of the hangar. Shishani headed to the steps and checked Kedzierski's body. He motioned for the others to get back on board. The pilot gestured to the tires as if to say he couldn't do anything, but Shishani was persistent.

As Maskadov put his foot on the bottom step Miranda pressed the trigger again, driving a round deep into the man's spine. It exited his chest, spraying the gleaming white paint with a red spray. The blonde returned to the doorway with a small submachinegun and began hosing the tree line, trying desperately to provide covering fire though the little gun was hopelessly outranged.

Miranda shifted her aim and fired a single shot, catching the woman's torso just under her third rib and rupturing her left lung. The round carried on through and out the right lung, eventually exiting the aircraft altogether on the opposite side and falling into the grass far on the east side of the runway. She dropped almost directly onto

Kedzierski.

With the ramp now blocked, the remaining passengers scrambled for cover on the far side. Still unsure of the location of their attacker, they shot hopelessly in the direction of the tree line with most rounds falling far short of Miranda's position.

Rodriguez jumped the bodies and made it on board the aircraft just as another round slapped into the aluminum frame of the doorway. Back at the hangar, the lead maintenance tech was dialing the police.

Dominguez, Shishani and the woman all ran for the far side of the plane; all trying to hide behind the narrow structure of the landing gear until they could figure out what to do. Soon, Rodriguez appeared in the doorway with a rifle of his own and laid prone, using the dead as his cover and rest.

He scanned the tree line hoping to see an indication of where Miranda might be. He knew if they couldn't get the sniper taken down there would be no chance of them getting off the runway alive. He grabbed his cell phone and tried to call the leader of the gang to see how far out their escort was, but nobody answered.

The woman made a run for the hangars with Dominguez on the opposite side of her. He was using the woman as a living shield to cover his own escape.

"Now that's just rude," Miranda said to herself as she led the pair with her scope.

The first shot was too far ahead and zipped by just in front of them. It was close enough that Dominguez stopped in his tracks, but the girl kept running.

"Gotcha." She pressed the trigger again.

The second shot impacted Dominguez high on the right chest. He dropped to the ground, but still struggled a bit. To Miranda's amazement, he stood back up, clutching at his ribs and began to scurry off, firing his pistol in the direction of her position.

She lobbed another round at the man, hitting him in the right hip and shattering his pelvis. Bone fragments and copper shards tore through the femoral artery as the bullet splintered his leg in the hip joint and he crumpled. Still, he tried to drag himself along. She watched for a moment as a crimson pool began to spread behind him. He was done for, he just didn't know it yet.

Suddenly the tree to her right began to splinter with gunfire. She had become so focused on taking down Dominguez that she forgot about Rodriguez back on the plane. She quickly switched her aim back to the aircraft and began pumping rounds into the doorway.

A heated exchange between marksmen began and ended just as abruptly when a lucky shot pierced the blonde woman's torso and careened upward, striking Rodriguez in the neck. With his head nearly severed by the round's energy, his fight was over.

She scanned the aircraft for a sign of Shishani. He wasn't hiding behind the landing gear, but she knew he couldn't have gone far. The area was too open for him to hide very well. Across the grass, on the far side of the runway, she spotted him in a shallow creek bed. He was crouched down and desperately trying to make a run for the hangar.

Meanwhile the employees of the airport were making mad dashes for their own vehicles. Soon the airport was abandoned with the exception of Miranda and Shishani. She still held the high ground, but he was putting distance between them.

Chapter 26

Mark stopped dead in his tracks and stared at Robinson. From behind him he could hear the approaching patrol closing in.

"Make your call, Adam," was all he could say. The young man had him if he wanted him and there was nothing Mark could do about it.

Robinson raised the pistols rapidly and fired two shots: directly past Himes and into the patrol that had rounded the corner behind him.

"Go," he said calmly, "I've got your back."

Without hesitation Himes turned the corner and headed for the steps. From behind him he could hear Robinson's pistols keeping up with his pace. The two men reached the stairwell as gunfire splintered the plaster above their heads.

Mark ran down to the first landing and swung around with the AR.

"C'mon!" he yelled to Robinson who raced to his level and then down the next flight, using the steps as cover for Himes to move.

A figure slid into the upper landing just as Mark turned to the steps. He swung the short rifle around and flipped the safety all the way around to the automatic mode and pressed the trigger. A spray of bullets filled the airspace at the top of the steps and the body of the gang member dropped to the floor. His forward momentum carried his body to the edge of the landing where his weapon dropped from his limp hands and fell to the bottom of the stairwell.

Mark bounded down the steps and past Robinson being mindful of the trip wire as he went. He took a covering position below and again called for Robinson to move.

As Adam launched himself over the trip wire the pursuers clamored down the steps behind them. He turned and fired into the group dropping another as they reached the second landing.

Himes and Robinson were at ground level and checking their avenue of escape. With the sun fully up now there was no hiding where they went.

"I got a car around that way," Robinson

said, "We get to it, we're gone. Follow me."

He peered out the doorway and stepped outside. As he did, Mark took aim at a pair of the men following them and squeezed the trigger again. At 600 rounds per minute, the 300 Blackout was like metallic rain in the stairwell, shredding both men before they could bring their own weapons to bear.

He lunged for the doorway and broke out into the sunshine, hot on Robinson's heels. As they rounded the corner the remainder of the team inside the building rushed down the steps and jumped over their fallen comrades. The second man, for whatever reason, landed as gracefully as Mark had on the roof that morning, sending himself tumbling down the steps and dislodging the detent pin from the device on the wall.

Mark and Robinson never slowed their pace as a rumble echoed from the structure. The anti-personnel device was loaded with a far heavier charge than needed and the entire stairwell paid the price. Both landings, the connecting steps, and all the people on them crumpled into a rubble pile at the bottom entangling weapons, bodies, steel and concrete together.

A block away Robinson gestured to the car he had waiting. A small grin had formed across his face. Mark had one as well, but his was still hidden beneath his mask. A few yards from the car another two man patrol stepped from the bushes and drew a bead on the fleeing men.

Mark raised his rifle just as Robinson swung his sidearms up. Shots echoed through the streets.

Miranda leapt from her position and began racing toward the main hangar building. She knew Shishani had gotten out of her effective range. The rifle could make the shot, but she doubted she could hit him. If she hurried, she could catch him at the building and take him out there.

"All those miles of running had better pay off," she thought as she poured every ounce of energy she could into making the distance.

She reached the back corner of the hangar as Shishani arrived at the terminal. With his pistol in his hand he began to sweep the buildings and spaces between, looking for a car, truck, bicycle, anything that could get him out of the facility.

Miranda silently crept around the building and went inside the hangar hiding in the corner behind a large tool box.

"*Now I'm here,*" she thought, "*What do I do?*"

A couple of minutes later and she could hear the door to the terminal building slam shut. He was on his way to the hangar. After a few seconds he stepped in the massive doorway and swept the room with his pistol. A pair of planes sat close to the entrance with the engine cowlings removed for service. Toward the rear was a smaller crop duster, but he would have to move the other two planes to get it out. As he moved across the room he spotted Miranda in the corner and swung his pistol up to meet her.

"You! You there! Come here!" he shouted with a heavy Chechen accent, "NOW!"

She stepped from her hiding place and her mind raced trying to decide what her next move should be.

"You can fly these planes?"

Miranda looked back at the man quizzically.

"You can fly these planes, yes?"

Miranda nodded her head.

He held the pistol in her direction and began to approach her.

"You help me and nothing will happen to you. You don't, I kill you. Understand?"

Again Miranda nodded her head.

He grabbed at her arm and began to drag her toward the plane closest to the doorway.

"Will this plane fly?"

Miranda nodded her head again as a plan began to take shape in her head.

He released her arm at the front of the aircraft and instructed her to begin prepping the plane for an immediate takeoff.

She stepped up on a small step ladder and began closing the cowling. As she did the sound of sirens could be heard in the distance. Shishani ran to the doorway and peered out. When he turned around to hurry Miranda's efforts along, he was greeted with a pair of nine millimeter hollow points to the face.

Shishani dropped to the floor of the hangar and Miranda policed up her brass casings, then streaked out the door to begin the long run back to the hide.

When she arrived at the hide site the first thing she noticed was that her rifle was gone.

Mark and Adam stood a few yards away from a pair of gang members that were obviously confused by what they saw.

There, in front of them, stood their patrol leader and the man that had been identified on the drone camera as the shooter that had killed their gang leader and head security man. Both were armed and looked to be working together. As the factors began to congeal, the man on the right raised his AK.

The seconds seemed to slow as Mark reacted to the threat. Robinson swung his pistols up as the second man brought his compact AR to his shoulder.

The AK fired followed immediately by Himes' AR. Robinson opened up with a pair of shots each from his handguns as the AR belched three rounds of its own.

The man with the AK dropped to the pavement followed closely by the man with the AR. Mark felt one of the bullets tug at his shirt tail as another streaked so close to his face that he could feel the air temperature rise. He looked to his left and saw Robinson beside him; a look of serious concern covered his face. He turned to face Mark and slid down to the pavement as he did.

Himes grabbed the young man under the arms and dragged him to the car as his shirt began to change color. He stuffed Adam in the back seat and leapt into the driver's side of the vehicle, tossing his bag in beside him.

Starting the car Himes stomped the gas and the custom Cutlass Supreme did the rest. He had never driven a car with 30 inch rims before and soon found out that cornering was not the vehicle's strongest, or most desirable, feature.

As he drove, he fumbled for his burn phone. He could already make out the sound of sirens in the distance and they were getting louder.

"What's up?"

"John. I need a medical evac NOW!"

"What? Are you OK?"

"It's not me. It's Robinson. He's been hit pretty bad. I'm in a donk on my way out right now. He's gonna need help right away."

"OK. Calm down and tell me where you are. I'll arrange something."

Mark read off the street names as he passed through the neighborhoods. Out of habit he was desperately trying to make his way back to his truck.

"NO! Do not go to your vehicle! I'm on my way. Pull over at the old warehouse on 11th and I will be there ASAP."

"OK. I'm stopping now. Hurry man. It's bad."

"Stay calm. Have you got anything you can use to slow the bleeding down?"

"Yeah, yeah I have a small first aid kit with some stuff in it. I'll see what I can do."

"On my way, buddy."

John hung up the phone while Mark scrambled through the duffel bag and produced a packet of Quick Clot gauze.

He tore it open and began packing the wounds in Robinson's chest at a frantic pace. With any luck it would stop the bleeding and he could be stabilized. Mark noticed the bag that Robinson carried was still slung over his shoulder. Through the open top he could see the old battered Bible peering out. Though Mark wasn't much of a religious man, he decided at that moment to have a prayer.

Miranda looked around the woods for the rifle. What could have happened to it? Nobody else knew where she was, did they?

A snap of a small twig to her left was all she needed to hear. She spun around and faced off with the pilot. Beside him stood the Latino woman that had been running with Dominguez. Over her shoulder was the M1A.

"Good morning, madam," he said with a smile, "It would seem that you have caused us a great deal of trouble today."

"Me? I'm just out for my daily run," Miranda smiled at the duo. She was kicking herself mentally for not taking the rifle with her and leaving the hide unattended.

"I see," the man continued, "Well your 'run' has cost us a very lucrative career as well as a fine aircraft. Fortunately, I think we can be at least partially compensated for that loss, with your cooperation, of course."

"What do you mean?"

"Well, a fine specimen of woman such as you will fetch a handsome price in many places around the world. Not as much as my dear Gulfstream, of course, but a fine price nonetheless."

He motioned for the woman to secure Miranda's hands and feet until they could figure out how to get all three of themselves out of the woods and back on track. The woman handed the rifle over to the pilot and began to approach

Miranda. An angry sneer crossed her face as she got closer and Miranda could tell it was about to get rough.

The woman brought her hand up to punch Miranda out, but she was met with a block and stomach jab instead. Before the woman could react, Miranda brought her knee up and drove it deep into the girl's abdomen pulling her down by the shoulders as she did so. The breath left the lungs and the woman crumpled. Miranda spun her around to face the pilot and, from behind the woman's back, unsnapped the Glock 43 from her holster.

She drove the weapon forward, the adrenaline surging through her system, and rapidly fired two rounds into the pilot's chest. She shoved the woman forward and aimed the compact pistol at her head. The woman turned and began to charge her, still furious and wanting to fight.

Miranda simply pulled the trigger twice again and the angry woman fell silent. Miranda quietly picked up the casings around her feet and dropped them into her pocket before retrieving the rifle. She broke everything down and stuffed it all in the bag as sirens filled the air in the distance all around the airport. She grabbed the burn phone and sent a text to Mark.

"I'm waiting."

John pulled up beside the Cutlass and practically jumped from the cruiser.

"Grab your stuff and go hide somewhere. I have an ambulance on the way. The area around the school should be flooded with cops right now. I'll take you wherever you need to go, but right now you need to be out of sight, Okay?"

Mark nodded in agreement and grabbed the duffel bag and darted for the nearest pile of pallets and drums he could find. As he squatted down he heard the ambulance arrive. He couldn't understand what was said from where he was, but he could tell John had an incredible lie that he was weaving like a master tapestry maker.

After a few minutes the medical team closed the doors and cranked the sirens. Adam was on his way to the hospital. Mark's phone chirped with an incoming message. It was Miranda. He had to go. He wasn't sure what had been happening on her end of the job, but he couldn't let her sit there for long. Someone would find her sooner or later.

Mark left the concealment of the garbage pile and approached John's car.

"You drove here in *this*?" John gestured to the car.

"Yeah. It doesn't look like much, but the sound system is incredible," Mark smiled, "Hey, man, take me to my truck. I have to go."

"Hop in."

Mark slid into the passenger seat and removed the mask for the first time all morning. He dropped the duffel bag on the floor board with the muzzle of the rifle still jutting out. It had cooled just enough that with a little extra effort he could now break it back down.

"Problems?" John said as he watched his friend struggling with the mechanism.

"Yeah, that's the problem with prototypes. I never tested it on multiple targets in a rapid fire setting. Too much heat makes the metal swell up."

He tucked it all back down in the bag and

sat back in the seat for a minute.

"Mark?"

"Yeah?"

"I gotta ask; is the car clean?"

"I wiped it down with some alcohol wipes from my first aid bag while I was waiting on you. It should be good."

John sat silently for a minute.

"Is he gonna make it?" Mark asked, almost afraid of the answer.

"Not sure. They said the Quick Clot helped control the bleeding, but he had already lost a lot. They wouldn't know until they got him stable. I told them to keep me up to date on his condition."

"Can you do me a favor?"

"Sure, man. What do you need?"

"After you drop me off, can you make sure he gets his bag?"

John pulled into the parking garage and drove Mark directly to his truck. Himes got out and pulled his keys out of his pocket, waving an exhausted salutation to his friend as he unlocked the door and got inside.

John rolled his window down.

"Say, we got calls out at the airport while you were in town. Do you want to explain that to me or is it a secret?"

"No secret. I hired an opening act."

Mark pulled up at the end of the fence row and scanned the field for any signs of Miranda. She was nowhere to be found. He began to worry about her. When he passed the entrance to the airport the police presence was heavy to say the least. He considered calling John to see if they had arrested her. That was an explanation he really didn't want to give.

Suddenly the bushes on the opposite side of the road began to rustle and Miranda emerged looking like she hadn't slept or eaten in days. She crossed in front of the truck and got in the passenger side.

"You OK?"

"Sorry. I've been a little sick over there. It's been a rough morning."

"Tell me about it," Mark replied sarcastically, "Why do you smell so bad?"

She rolled her head toward him and half smiled, "One thing you didn't tell me when you dropped me off this morning in the dark."

"Oh? What's that?"

"This fence row? It's on the edge of a cow pasture."

Mark shot her a glance and then looked at her feet. Both of her hiking boots were completely covered, up onto her pant legs, with a thick coating of manure.

"Yeah," he grumbled, "It happens."

Chapter 26

Adam Robinson lay quietly with his head on the pillow; a smile across his face despite all he had been through. In his hands he held his Bible; an old, battered reminder of the man he used to be and the man he had become.

A few feet away sat James and Jenny. James was as stoic as ever while Jenny reflected the emotional stress that she endured.

As Mark approached he could see James' nostrils flare a bit and a smile barely cross his face.

"Help me up, Jenny, I need to go to the bathroom for a minute," he said.

Mark took the cue as he, John and Miranda followed the old veteran out of the room.

"How are you doing, son?"

"As well as can be expected, Corporal. Yourself?"

"Oh, we'll make it," he said. The expression on his face never changed despite his nephew, his son, lying in the next room.

"Bring company, did you?"

"Yes, sir. These are my friends, John and Miranda. They're both here at my request. John is the one that got Adam to the hospital."

"My thanks to you. I appreciate everything you've done to get my boy back home."

"Yes sir. I'm just sorry it didn't work out as well as we had hoped," John replied.

A man appeared behind James and placed a hand on the old man's shoulder.

"Mr. Carver? We're ready."

"Thank you," he said and turned back to Mark, "Jenny and I have thought about what you said at our last meeting. We've decided to take some of the money we have been putting aside and set up a college scholarship fund for kids in the neighborhood. It won't be much, but maybe we can help someone else from taking the same steps Adam did. I appreciate the notion. Excuse me. I'd better go back inside. And stop calling me 'sir.'"

Mark shook the man's hand and watched

as he resumed his seat beside his wife. The casket was soon closed and the funeral for Adam Lee Robinson began.

Chapter 27

"Hello?"

"I think we have everything figured out," John said.

Mark sat up on his stool in the workshop.

"OK. What have you got?"

"Well, the rewards for all of the bad guys and their cronies came to just over $750,000. It took a lot of bargaining and manipulating by the Chief, but he managed to get $600,000 of it secured. There was a lot of resistance because some very big organizations really wanted those fine folks to stand trial. I swear, the Chief has a future in politics if he ever decides to quit his job.

"Anyway, the 'official' story is that the bad guys were taken out through a precision strike by our SWAT team after weeks of exhaustive planning. The SWAT guys are getting the credit, but they are being told it was a covert, multi departmental DHS sting and it is completely hush hush.

It isn't to be discussed due to the long reaching connections the criminals had.

"The reward money is going to be split into two parts. One third will go to the Adam Robinson Scholarship fund. The remaining two thirds are going to be set up in a dummy account that only you will have access to. Will that work?"

"That should be fine, John. Tell the Chief 'thank you' for all his leg work on keeping the names out of it. I don't want to know what he did or how, but I appreciate it. Any idea when the money will be available?"

"It will take a couple of weeks for all the approvals and transfers. After that it's all on you. The department will receive the official access, but it will be turned over to you as soon as it's complete."

"Thanks, John," Mark stretched a bit, yawning into the phone as he did.

"Tired?"

"Yeah, my brain is a little fried trying to figure out improvements to this take down rifle. After the way it seized up on me I started making notes on what to change. I have a lot of work to do.

"Not to change the subject, but what time do you leave?"

"Not sure," John said, "Miranda's on the phone with her dad right now. We're packing; I'm just not sure about the details. All I know is that she is picking me up to go to the airport in a couple of hours."

"Yes, Dad, he's a nice guy. As a matter of fact, he's a great guy. You'll like him, I know you will," Miranda smiled into the phone, "So, can you have Andrew pick us up at the airport? Ok. That will be great. I can't wait to see you both. Alright. We'll see you in a few hours, then. I love you."

Miranda finished packing her two small bags and summoned Chauncey into his travel crate. She loaded the car and was shortly on her way to John's place.

Before long she stepped up to the apartment door, ringing the bell with a giddy enthusiasm. John swung the door open wide and smiled as the two embraced with a passionate kiss.

"Gear up, Mr. Thompson, we have a trip to take," she said with a smile.

John grabbed his bag and headed for the door. Miranda followed closely behind, locking the apartment as he stepped out.

After several minutes of driving they arrived at McClendon Field. Miranda locked her car up and the pair stepped into the office area. The little man at the counter shot her a curious glance as she smiled to him.

"Finally decided to take that trip, ma'am?"

"Yes. Everything's been arranged. Thank you for letting me leave my car here for a few days."

"No problem. It should be fine," he smiled and went back to his paperwork.

Miranda stepped out the back door of the terminal and scanned the runway. Beside the hangar sat the Gulfstream with the landing gear still unrepaired and several bullet holes blemishing the gleaming white paint of the right side.

As she stood there the distinctive whine of

Pratt and Whitney engines could be heard and soon a Cessna Citation came rolling to a stop in front of them. The stairway opened as the pilot stepped out and approached Miranda.

"Are you ready, Miss Ashcroft?" he asked.

"Yes, Andrew. Thank you for picking us up."

John's jaw dropped as she nodded and the man collected their belongings.

"We…we need to talk, sweetie," was all he could say.

"Yeah. Yeah, we do."

ALSO FROM BRIAN CHEATHAM

REDUCTION

ISBN:
978-1-546-93092-1
Book #1 of the
Reduction Saga

Mark Himes was an average guy with an average life. That life is threatened when the economy turns for the worst and his plant closes. Out of a job and desperate for regular work, Himes turns to a friend for advice. The answer he gets is unexpected, and dangerous. Himes must choose to struggle with finding work or act as an assassin for law enforcement to curb the growing crime rate in the city. He would be working outside the law, for the law. How far would one man go to provide for his family?

Made in the USA
Columbia, SC
18 December 2017